SLEEPLESS NIGHT

MARGRIET DE MOOR

Translated from the Dutch by David Doherty

NEW VESSEL PRESS
NEW YORK

New Vessel Press

www.newvesselpress.com

First published in Dutch as *Slapeloze nacht*
Copyright © 2016 Margriet de Moor.
Published by De Bezige Bij, Amsterdam.
Translation Copyright © 2019 David Doherty

The publisher gratefully acknowledges the support
of the Dutch Foundation for Literature.

N ederlands
letterenfonds
dutch foundation
for literature

Library of Congress Cataloging-in-Publication Data
De Moor, Margriet
[Slapeloze nacht. English]
Sleepless Night/ Margriet de Moor; translation by David Doherty.
p. cm.
ISBN 978-1-939931-69-6
Library of Congress Control Number 2018963552
I. The Netherlands—Fiction

SLEEPLESS NIGHT

I t's another of those nights. A night to live through,
without sleep.

For years now, I have been in the habit of getting up. As a novice, this was something I did not do. I
stayed under the covers, flinging myself from one side
of the bed to the other, and listened for the striking of
the clock. Odd, when you think about it. All you want
is to slip away, into the countless hours, the immense
space where the ticking of time only occurs by way
of a joke, but instead you lie there muttering, "One
... two ... three already, damn it!" And by an easterly
wind, you hear your sentence confirmed seconds later

7

by a faint clang from the village steeple. More chime than church bell. I would often listen to the trains, too. And it struck me that while all of creation lay still at this hour, these nocturnal transports rolled on, uninterrupted. In resignation or in panic, I would feel the wheels rumble even before I heard them, the vibration intensifying as it burrowed through fields and ditches to latch onto the dresser mirror, which would begin to rattle unbearably. What was it that had to be carried with such stealth across the silent country?

What I do now is get up and make my way barefoot down the unlit stairs. Anatole, my mongrel German shepherd, hears me coming and knows what to expect. By the time I step into the kitchen and switch on the light, the dog has heaved himself up and is stretching his stiff legs. I take out the flour, the eggs, the hand mixer, two bowls—one big, one small—and begin without hesitation. I never have to think what to make. I just know. Shortbread cookies. Apple cake. Breton ham pie.

I am grateful to my husband for installing the oven at eye level when he equipped the kitchen. My eye level. Just as he chivalrously made the kitchen counter to suit my height and not his, which—as I came to learn—was six feet four and a half.

When it is time to slide the cake pan or baking tray into the preheated oven, I set the kitchen timer.

This is essential. Once I have entered the dark living room in the company of Anatole, I lose all sense of temperature, aroma, and the time needed for a perfect golden-brown crust. From a corner of the room, I hear the dog sink to the floor with a smack and I begin to walk.

I am grateful to my husband for this soft wooden floor, laid with his own two hands. I know that he salvaged these planks of oak from a scrapyard. I even know that the wood originally came from the Heide Hotel, an old hunting lodge. I walk a floor for which a tidy sum was once paid. As he worked away in the living room—I can still hear the short, intense blasts of hammering—I was running an angled paintbrush along the frame of the door that leads down to the cellar. I remember how pleased I was with the color, a grayish green that even now, almost fifteen years later, still seems just right. I recall the stiffness in my fingers when the paint that had dripped down the side of the brush began to dry. I didn't have much space to work in. I see very clearly that the sweep of my clumsy efforts was hemmed in by a pile of secondhand chairs and boxes crammed with wedding gifts. While the Chinese bowls, the tablecloth embroidered with irises, the cocktail shaker, and goodness knows what else are items I still possess and see almost every day, Ton, my young husband, has vanished without a trace. The look on his face. The remarks he made from the living room.

"Clear varnish might be best after all."

"Tea? Or a beer?"

"You'll never guess who I ran into this morning."

"Over halfway done and moving along."

"Sure. But it's not what you're thinking."

Along those lines. Accompanied perhaps by a whistled tune or a burst of laughter. I can stick my fingers in my ears and bring the remarks to mind. But they are words without intonation, spoken with a mouthful of sand. As he went about this task, I neglected to notice my husband.

Walking the floor of the darkened living room calms me. There is nothing more to it than that. I sleepwalk over the bands of oak, which I would swear have grown warmer with the passing of the years and the friction of my footsteps. And there is no doubt that the effect I achieve bears more than a passing resemblance to the workings of dreams. The sense of melting into things hidden or shoved aside.

I usually glance at the mirror as I pass. On a clear night, strange, haggard eyes meet mine and sometimes I can make out the line of dark-brown hair, cut along the jawline. By the window, I spend a moment or two looking out on the land. My land. The place I inherited. It rises up to meet me, a steepish slope that still brings to mind the swell of the sea. Depending on the season, a wave of corn, charred leaves, or raw, black earth seems poised to sweep away the farm, forming its own premature horizon beyond which the fields roll down to the village, out of view.

On a night like this, it's unusual for sleep to pass me by. An hour must have elapsed since I lifted the heavy arm off me. How much does an arm weigh, I wondered, gauging as I raised it. Thirteen pounds? Fifteen perhaps? He carried on sleeping, an amiable expression on his face. Sleeping so soundly in a strange bed. It has long since ceased to surprise me; they all do it. I folded his arm, placed his fist next to his cheek, and slid away from him. "Butter squares sprinkled with cinnamon" popped into my head, as I felt my way down the stairs.

I arrive at the window, press my brow to the glass, and look outside. Clearer than ever tonight, the swell rises up to meet me. An ice-pale moonlit sea. It's been a strange week in these parts. First the fields were buried under two feet of snow, then came a day of mild rain that failed to wash them clean before the wind swept in and the temperature plummeted to twelve below freezing. A brittle crest of shoveled snow lines the path in front of the house, and with next to no effort I recall my feet sloshing through tepid, yellow-tinged foam. I hail from the coast; as a child the stink of farmland used to fill me with dread.

The locals all expected me to pack up and leave after the funeral. Back to the life I had left not so long before. What was there for me now, here on this land? The shameful death lent no luster to my newfound state, not a glimmer of tragic glory.

"You have to stay," Lucia had said. "That's all. Just stay."

She was sitting on the kitchen windowsill and I remember fretting that she might lean back and rest her hand on the scales. They were my pride and joy, a mechanism sensitive enough to weigh flour or salt to a fraction of an ounce. What my sister-in-law did not know was that it had been settled since my first wakeful night: I could not leave this place. It was barely even a decision. This house is where I will stay. And as for the land, I will sell it to my neighbors, Braams and Pepping.

It was a Saturday afternoon, the first since the commotion and fuss of the funeral. Other than Lucia, no one had dropped by that day. I had not been pitied or questioned. For some reason no mail had been delivered. The telephone had not rung once. My instinct told me that this was the beginning of a deeper stillness, one that would stay with me from now on. The world had deliberately left me alone with it today, as with a strange creature that had invaded my home, a snake or a wild colt. I had not been smart enough to keep it outside and no one would be crazy enough to share the chore of tending to it. That Saturday I had already begun to understand that I would have to find my own way to approach this stillness, a way to tame it and raise it.

"And if they're not in a position to buy the land, Braams and Pepping will be all too happy to lease it from you," my sister-in-law continued firmly.

Out of friendship and common courtesy, I looked at her. My eyes narrowed, I gave a slight nod and must have given the impression that I was mulling over what she had said. Instead, I found myself wondering whether she resembled her brother. It had never occurred to me before. His build, of course, had never been so slender. His hair couldn't have been as red and nowhere near as full and glossy. But there was something about the eyes. She's been through the mill this week, her blouse is soiled, ringed with sweat—she must have been sweltering yesterday or the day before—but there's an ease in the way she looks at me. And those eyelashes, something that always tickles me about redheads, so light and densely planted, almost birdlike. The look of someone who has no time for nonsense, I thought, and no time at all for self-pity.

"It's worth thinking about," I mumbled.

With the passing of the years, the village has resigned itself to my staying.

The timer goes off. Even from behind two closed doors, the infernal noise never fails to make me jump. Anatole gets up and we return to the kitchen. I remove the tray from the oven. The cake has turned out splendidly, and with the greatest of care, I slice it into two-inch squares. Once I have washed the dishes and wiped the counter, I put down a bowl of water for the dog. Knowing I have over half the night ahead of me and that the dough needs to rise for an hour, I decide there is still time for a Russian Bundt cake. Then it dawns on me that we took the vodka upstairs with us after dinner. Like a veteran married couple intent on rounding off the evening in style, we got up from the table at around eleven. I climbed the stairs behind him, carrying two slim, elegant glasses.

I need the booze for the cake I'm going to make.

Bottle in hand, I pause a moment by the bed. In his sleep, he has pulled the covers half over his head. The light from the reading lamp shines sidelong on the rumpled sheet. Looking more closely, I see the folds gently rise and fall. Rising and falling to the rhythm of audible breathing, the unmistakable slumber of a man after a hard day's work.

I know the feeling. I am usually worn-out myself. It is almost impossible to put into words how tiring it is to spend a day with someone you don't know. Many's the time I could barely keep my eyes open until that steady rhythm kicked in, the sound that all was well and I, too, could roll over.

It's a good system. Lucia and I came up with it years ago, a time when alarming things began to happen to me. I would get up in the morning and not be able to move my hands. Stiff as grappling hooks they were, rigid fingers spread wide for fifteen minutes, some days for up to an hour. Worse still was the discoloration and puffiness in my face, every hollow filled—the eye sockets, the curve between jaw and neck. The lines that speak of character, that express much more than the color of the eyes, much more than the shape of the lips, were bulked out under taut skin. Pressing my fingertips to my face, I could feel the thickness beneath. It did not hurt.

"You've bolted down a hole and you won't come out," Lucia said. "Not even to come up for air. It's an insult to your lust for life! Your elemental needs!"

She smoked cigarillos back then, strode around in her riding breeches and an olive-brown Shetland wool sweater. Everything about her—I sensed it all too clearly in the way she looked and moved, even in the way she sat hunched and smoking on the little basket chair, chin on her knees—was shot through with sexual abandon, and had been since the young Martens lad had moved in with her a few months earlier.

All I could do was agree despondently.

"This convent existence is making my body livid."

"A nun's best-kept secret."

It took us the rest of the afternoon to draft the personal ad we placed in *de Volkskrant*. It wound up being a single sentence, albeit one that left little to the imagination.

I hear the dog snuffling from one end of the hallway to the other. He is not used to me disappearing upstairs between acts. But it's pleasant to linger, listening to the breathing, looking down at the half-hidden face, and as I do, it begins to dawn on me why I have so little need of sleep. I am not tired at all. What should have been a taxing day, drawing on all my reserves to face off with a complete stranger, in fact turned out to be a self-evident, almost casual affair. It was with a cool air of familiarity that this man came walking up to me this morning.

The bustle at the station was not the agreeable kind. There were lines at the ticket counters, unusual for a Saturday. In the underpass between platforms three and four, it was all I could do to hold steady amid the surge of travelers rushing single-mindedly in the opposite direction. After a short, solitary wait on the platform for the 10:10 from Zwolle, an announcement came crackling over the speakers and, before I knew what was happening, people came scurrying from all directions. Service was disrupted. Frozen switches. Ice clinging to overhead lines. I joined the rest, staring into the mist at the blurred red glow of the signals down by the level crossing.

A train pulled in. The doors clunked open and were stormed in an instant. Only then did it dawn on me that we had forgotten to agree on a sign, a way of recognizing each other. Not that this worried me. I continued to lean quietly against the stone balustrade at the top of the stairs.

He must have alighted from a front carriage and made no attempt to hurry through the crowd. He simply remained behind when the train departed. A man in his forties—this I already knew—lean in the face, his receding hairline just the right side of attractive. In a long brown coat that had seemingly shrugged off every fashion of the past fifteen years, he walked up to me.

We shook hands. Spoke our names in clouds of breath.

"How was your trip?" I asked.

"Not bad, all told. Left at eight. Snow in Roermond. We were the other side of Eindhoven before it started to get light. Ground to a halt for half an hour, couldn't tell you where. Fields either side."

A man from the South without a southern accent. He spoke like my father, my brothers, my uncles.

"Were you raised in the North by any chance?" I ventured. "Bulb-growing country?"

"Lived up Bloemendaal way till I turned twenty. But

what I'm wondering"—he looked around and his eyes lit upon the sign for the station cafeteria—"is whether they serve a decent cup of coffee around here."

Inside it was quiet and warm. The place was run by a no-nonsense character who was of the opinion that travelers should have a stove around which to gather. We sat down next to a cast-iron colossus that had been equipped with a gas burner. There, enveloped in the aroma of strong tobacco, coffee, and almond cakes still warm from the oven, we looked out at the coming and going of the trains, and at the passengers who, in thrall to the wintry conditions, seemed desperately jittery about reaching their destinations.

We began hunting for our smokes. He thrust one hand deep into a brown coat pocket and pulled out a lighter and a pack of cigarettes. I decided to have one of his. He held out a flame.

It's something I always look at in a man, a wrist exposed as it emerges from the sleeve of a jacket, or better still, an overcoat. That seemingly insignificant contrast between body and clothing; you need an eye for such things, of course, a feel for them, too, but I maintain that the casual flexing of a wrist dusted with reddish hair, or the transition from a wiry arm to a nervous hand, speaks a language all its own. A plain language, less prone to dissembling than the movements of the lips or the line of the body as a whole.

Ton used to love helping me in the kitchen. We cooked impulsively, hurriedly. Macaroni, chicken and rice—simple, tasty meals. Yet the turn of his hand as he opened a can of beans is an image I can no longer bring to mind.

He looked at me with frank curiosity.

"So you teach at a village school," he said, picking up a strand from my letter. As good an opening as any.

My turn.

"Yes. Going on fifteen years now. Fourth grade. The nicest age to teach, if you ask me. Not much harm you can do. The kids can already read, write, add and subtract, and that's what they came for in the first place. What about you?"

"I'm an editor for a historical encyclopedia."

"Oh, that must be fun," I said cheerfully. "Everything that's ever happened passes before your eyes. A man who's concerned with the facts."

He returned my sly grin.

"How they come and then go when they've had their time," I mused.

"Mmm," he replied. "You'd be surprised how fast history goes to seed. It's in constant need of sprucing up."

We shared a friendly gaze. I asked if the job gave him much satisfaction.

"Well, you know, it's work."

Our attention was caught by a bunch of young skaters in metallic-blue skin suits, as they charged up the stairs to the platform. In an all-or-nothing bid to make their connection, they leaped onto the tracks and only just managed to scramble onto the far platform as the train pulled in. Furious shouts erupted from all directions and the train let out a plaintive hoot. The stationmaster came storming past.

An old lady dozing at a table strewn with newspapers woke with a start, put on her glasses, and shot us an embittered look.

"You people nowadays think of no one but yourselves!" she shouted, trembling.

Calm settled in once more. Again, I felt his eyes on me. Though it had never occurred to me that we might make each other's acquaintance by this hulking stove, the situation was one I knew well. The questioning had begun and was set to continue for the remainder of the day.

I looked at him candidly. Assiduously even. As a schoolgirl I would readily volunteer answers during class tests. And however tenuous my grasp of what we were supposed to have learned, as often as not I would hit the nail on the head. That willingness has never left me. I am happy to furnish information. Whether I'm accosted by a traffic cop, in a department store, on a train. What would you like to know? I have no secrets.

As far as I'm concerned, the facts of my life are a matter of public record.

He asked me if I had been alone a long time and I nodded.

"Thirteen years and six months."

"Then your marriage can't have lasted long."

"Oh, I wouldn't say that. Over fourteen months. From July 1970 till the following September."

The time had come to explain—this, too, had become second nature—that I was not a divorcée but a widow. As he listened, without making a show of his attentiveness, I drew back the curtain on the drama that had taken place one late summer evening. Shortly before eight o'clock, they later assured me, my twenty-five-year-old husband, wearing jeans, linen shoes, and a blue T-shirt—all perfectly ordinary, you see—walked to the greenhouse where he had set up an experimental installation for growing chicory under glass, where roots that came direct from the Northeast Polder were stacked in trays without so much as a grain of soil and stored for one month at 4 degrees Celsius in a semblance of winter before being ripened in a stream of oxygenated water—incredible when you think about it, a year and a half of natural growth reduced to just three months—and there, at the far end of the greenhouse, my husband took his own life by shooting himself in the head with a 9mm Luger. The weather, like every other day that September week, had been mild, windless. The villagers had been busy getting ready for the big annual livestock show, the "Stock Pile," as they jokingly called it.

The men I meet all respond differently, but they are seldom shocked or surprised. I think this is because I am a stranger to them. The things that happen to strangers have only a limited degree of reality. Vaguer than dreams or stories. Vaguer than a jumbled movie plotline. A friend once confided in me that a shared acquaintance, someone we hardly knew—you remember, the guy who played the organ so beautifully at that summer concert in the parish church—was about to be admitted to the hospital for open-heart surgery, and there was every chance he would not survive. Back in the solitude of my student digs, I must have sobbed out loud for a good thirty minutes before I looked at myself in the mirror. Yet now, as I relate what happened on the fringes of my own life, my face remains cold and I partake in the impassiveness of my listeners.

Some want to know how he came by the Luger.

"It was a family heirloom. The weapon his father used in the resistance. A sacred object, burnished by wartime heroism."

"But did he know how to handle it? And where did he get the ammunition?"

"Yes, everyone wondered about that."

One man narrowed his eyes and inquired whether he had put the barrel in his mouth or—

"No," I cut him short. "The side of the head." And pressed a finger to my temple. "A bullet fired at such close range comes out the other side. Took them a long time to find. It had rolled into the sorting machine."

"Why did he do it?" Quite a few ask that question, as you might expect.

It is one to which I have no answer. And for this I am genuinely sorry. It's a very unpleasant sensation, to be left speechless on that point. Every appeal to my knowledge, my intuition, my knack for inspired associations, has been in vain. I cannot tell a single soul what possessed my husband in the final moments of his life. And every now and then I find myself on the receiving end of the look that hit me hardest as the well-meaning schoolgirl I once was: reproach. I have messed up. The toughest word from the dictation is lost beneath an inkblot the size of a beetle. I did my best but memorized the wrong chapter. Feeling small, I lower my eyes.

He looked at me earnestly but asked no questions. We sat silently a while. The crowds out on the platforms seemed to be thinning. A train slid soundlessly from view behind the lace curtain. The old lady had nodded off again over her newspaper, one hand outstretched in a fingerless glove, as if begging for alms.

He stood up, plucked the empty cup from my hand, and took it over to the counter with his. I watched and felt a restlessness take hold.

This was supposed to be another of those days when I dish up the facts without a flicker of surprise. As I had done for years. The fulfillment, the soothing of my "elemental needs" was now accompanied by a phenomenon to which I had grown attached: saying my piece. I watched as my companion ordered fresh coffee and bargained for a jug of hot milk instead of a packet. I must have already told him how much I preferred the real thing to powder. The heat from the stove was intense. My hands lay pale and damp in my lap. Hands that in no time had turned soft and supple again, once the protocol initiated by Lucia and me had begun to work its magic. Not a trace of the grappling hooks they had once been. The cure had been all but instant. My face had slimmed, my body, too, and both seemed to hold a certain appeal.

On one side, the hem of his coat was hanging lower than the other. I was unable to take my eyes off it, but why? It was a thick brown coat like countless others; I pictured him stowing it away for the summer and retrieving it with a contented smile as autumn set in. What was so riveting about that?

A special calm is needed to make this dough. It's wise to have everything on hand before you start. Flour. Salt. Sugar. I take the big bowl, dissolve the yeast in milk. You knead the mixture for five minutes first, and only then do you add the eggs. From that moment on, you have to be careful. Yeast and eggs are extremely volatile ingredients. They make the mixture swell. They give off gases. And, a process which never fails to astound me, they double the original volume. I start by raking my fingers firmly through the ingredients.

It's nonsense, of course, to suppose that I do not

remember Ton. Every woman remembers her husband. Things happened. Pleasant things, most likely, natural, too—so natural they seemed to happen of their own accord and left no impression. On Sundays, we were in the habit of having breakfast under the pear trees. We sat on rickety antique chairs. Ton boiled the eggs and served them up in an oven glove to keep them warm. How often would it have been? A summer long, a handful of times? I laid a garland of nasturtium around his plate, trickled honey into the calyxes of the edible flowers. Why? Out of love? Some sentimental notion? Because that morning my hair had fallen into a fetching wave?

I press the base of my thumb into the dough. The surface still crumbles slightly. With slow, steady movements, I squeeze the mass together. I work in silence. It's unthinkable that the mixer might shred the intense stillness of the night. The machine stands next to the stove, gathering grease and dust. I might as well toss it out altogether, for even during the day, when there could be no objection to using it, the notion never enters my head. Its nerve-jangling din is superfluous in any case. My fingers do the job as well as any pulsating dough hook, if not better. It's simply a matter of making sure your hands don't get too warm and turn the mixture gummy.

Ton. His name was Ton. Not a name that struck

a chord with me, it was just a good fit. It matched the way he walked and talked, the blue sweater he draped around my shoulders that day we went sailing. Oh, when I think of the ease with which he turned the boat into the howling wind and brought us to a clean halt six inches from the pier. By that time my lips were chewed raw; I tasted blood for hours.

I turn on the faucet and rinse my hands with cold water. Then I dust the counter with flour. It is an old-fashioned granite surface. The stone was still free of cracks, and Ton and I saw no need to replace it with stainless steel. It is a source of pleasure to me now. It's true what they say, the coolness held in a slab of nature never disappears entirely.

This is where things get ugly. I plant my feet wider apart and take a deep breath. In the dead of night, I begin to pound away, slamming my fists into the pale, pliant lump in front of me. Just as well there's not another living soul around to witness this. It's like a scene from a nightmare, one of those silent terrors that leave you swallowed up by some unreal entity, clingy and elastic. Of course I remember my husband. All I have to do is start at the beginning, with an image I can call to mind effortlessly, at any given moment.

Almost everyone advised me not to go and see him.

"It's better to remember him the way he was." My mother was the first to say these words.

I nodded. She was right, that would be best. Probably. The inhuman weight of this viewpoint did not press upon me till much later.

It was the day after what everyone had quickly started to refer to as the accident. My mother and I were sitting opposite each other, slightly ill at ease in the cold leather armchairs by the windows. I felt ashamed of not having dressed. It was almost noon and the hem of my nightgown lay crumpled across my knees.

My mother is a formidable woman who has raised three children. I have never known her to wear anything other than voluminous floral dresses. She came over as soon as she heard. Her red station wagon had pulled up in front of the house before nine. I asked her how she remembered my father. This was a moment for the truth and she answered truthfully: the first time she had seen him naked. It had been the morning after, at the hotel. As she lay in bed, he had gotten up and opened the curtains. The sunlight of a foreign land cascaded over him.

"Pale and sturdy he was, as he strode across the floor."

She looked at me with a tinge of melancholy and hastened to assure me that she often pictured him at his desk, too, tallying up the figures he had just jotted down in a twenty-year-old cash ledger with an unsteady, freckled hand.

Lucia arrived that afternoon. Absorbed in the solemn task of the obituary notice, I was sitting at the table with my eldest brother when I saw her pass the front window. At that exact moment, elusive fragments of mourning, regret, and fondness formed phrases that rose up inside me, and my brother nodded and began scribbling furiously. I had only caught a glimpse of her, but I knew right away. She had seen him. She had driven to the funeral home in the next village and looked down at the corpse of her brother. I knew what she had come to propose. And in my mind, I had already agreed. Soon I'll be sitting next to her in the car, and perhaps she'll drive more calmly than usual, but in no time, we'll have left behind this sunny village, strung with bunting. We will have to take a detour. The Brink is closed off for the livestock show.

Lucia walked into the room and, in that matter-of-fact way of hers, chimed in where my thoughts had left off.

"Unless you see him, you'll spend your whole life not wanting to believe it."

My mother handed her a cup of coffee, which she drank standing up. Every now and then she took a step toward the table to tap her cigarette on the rim of the ashtray. Her eyelids were a little swollen, but there was nothing special in that. September always seemed to land her with some allergy or other. She looked at me and said in her usual offhand way, "It really isn't that bad, you know."

We were just about to drive off when two men, total strangers to me, came walking up the path. Feeling dazed, I got back out of the car. They took hold of my hands and began to intone guttural condolences. They had tears in their eyes and so I did my best to look as sympathetic and heartening as possible. Please, you're welcome, go right in, I gestured, in the vague hope that my brother might offer them a cigar.

Sure enough, we were there in no time.

L ooking back, it's the fullness of the days that surprises me most. I was never alone. After an opening salvo of tears and questions, everyone who stopped by was determined to stick around and help out. I came up with all kinds of chores. Copying out addresses, feeding the rabbits. An insane amount of coffee was made.

People thought I looked pale, that my eyes shone unnaturally. Above all, they agreed that I was being far too brave. Shortly after midday, I was persuaded to take a nap. Someone slipped off my shoes. The dark-red curtains were drawn. I promptly fell asleep and dreamed, as I often did when I slept during the day, that I was being made love to expertly by a total stranger. Without feeling the least surprise, I let myself be woken by the rather dour woman who drove the mobile library through the village on Wednesdays, and one minute later I was talking to a policeman, explaining unasked that my marriage had been a happy one.

My mother offered to stay for a day or two, and got settled up in the attic. Even so, a young cousin of Ton's decided on the second evening, when things were still very chaotic, that she would share my bed to spare me the pain of waking in the dark to an empty space under the covers. I raised no objection.

The girl had an endearing way of sleeping. For minutes on end she rolled from one side to the other until her fine-boned body found just the right curve. By this time, her blond hair, which I admired greatly, had fanned out over my face and every stitch of bedclothes had slid to the floor on her side of the bed. Not that it mattered. The sultry afternoon had brewed up a rainstorm that showed little sign of letting up. The air that flowed into the house steeped everything— towels, sheets, pillowcases—in a sticky kind of sweat, and it was no hardship to lie in bed uncovered. The girl was fast asleep and I listened in wonder to the gentle quivering in her nose and throat. It did not seem to disturb her. Ton always lay close to me, on his side, one arm crooked under my pillow. While obviously not as motionless as I had found him that afternoon, he was always peaceful and still when he slept. You barely even noticed he was there.

"What a hulking great thing!" I said to Lucia, as soon as we entered.

The coffin lay in a spotless, air-conditioned room, all filtered light and flickering candles.

"Well, they measured him exactly," Lucia said. "Six feet four and a half. I'm sure they know their stuff."

I walked over without looking, let my hand glide over the wood. Young birch, I reckoned. A high-gloss varnish always gives that speckled effect. But then I saw that Lucia was right. Ton lay practically wedged in cream-white satin. Stupid of me, I thought, to give the undertakers those navy-blue pants for him this morning. He had never worn them, and besides, they were much too warm for this time of year. Hardly the burial clothes of a young farmer. Seeing that the jacket had ridden up a little at the shoulders, I took hold of the seams on either side and gave a careful tug with both hands. To no avail; there was barely any slack. I leaned closer.

The face consisted of a large, round jaw, two expanses of cheek shaved smooth as can be, and a mouth that had been colored in. The eyes were closed, expressionless, of course, but at an odd angle to one another. The right eye seemed to have sunk slightly.

Looking up, my gaze met Lucia's and I smiled as if to say, You were right, it's not that bad.

Then I looked again. This was not a face anyone would want to capture in a portrait. A few days earlier it might have been an option. Someone could have snapped a handsome likeness of a man who had yet to reach his prime. I could have had it enlarged. The lines, the shadows, the slight asymmetry would have hinted at the things that had occurred through the years, and most definitely at everything still to come. All pointless now. The ripples of a life story had disappeared completely from this face. Run aground on one absurd detail: the moment when that little dent had appeared in the right side of his head.

After eight in the evening.

I nudged open the side door of the school with my elbow and carried the tray bearing cups and a thermos jug out onto the square. As the youngest teacher, I had offered to fix coffee. An open house at the school was part of the festivities for the livestock show, and we were busy putting together an exhibition of the children's drawings. The village was buzzing. Elderly women held court at the school entrance, watching their children and grandchildren string streamers from one tree to another, fence off the Brink, and line up straw bales to mark the course for the tilt-at-the-ring contest that was to run from the milk plant all the way to the village pub. They were wondering why on earth it was taking their daughters so long to brew a pot of coffee. And there I came, bustling to the rescue across the playground, the evening air still heavy with heat. And as I put the tray on the table, in the shade of the three poplar trees whose intertwined trunks always reminded me of a dromedary's legs, Ton must have been heading down to the greenhouse.

The big chicory greenhouse is quite a distance from the house. Head straight across the land where, at that time of year, the corn would have been five feet tall. Turn right at the end and there's the greenhouse, over by the potato field that belongs to Braams, who at that hour can always be found sitting against the wall of his outbuilding, having a smoke. Chicory grows in the soil. That's why the greenhouse has to be warm and muggy. That's why it has to be dark. A heavy rubber curtain hangs by the door and lets in no light. I always found it a pleasant place to be. The sound of the water being continually pumped past the roots through a network of PVC pipes was especially pleasing. A clattering, cheerful sound.

I walked back into the school building to round up my colleagues for coffee. In passing, my eyes lingered on the drawings and it struck me that, as the children grew older, what they drew seemed more cautious and restrained, emptier somehow. The children from my class drew thin tables, thin chairs, a flat cat. Never a dog. I picked up a sheet of paper on which a six-year-old had conjured up a magnificent monster in blotches of red and black. "All head and legs," said one of the other teachers, coming up behind me. "He's still at the schematic stage." I walked over and pinned it up on the board. There! And meanwhile Ton must have been regulating the oxygen, salt, and minerals in the water, as young Martens and his brother discovered the next morning when they came to help out in the greenhouse as usual—I could not believe it, but they were adamant: he must have taken care of the nutrient levels that evening. And having done this, he drew the heavy curtain between him and the pitch darkness a little to one side.

I pressed a thumbtack into the paper.

Out back, Braams was roused from his doze by a loud, sharp noise and knew immediately that it was malign.

The fever of sleeplessness drives people to do the strangest things. They whisper poems that appear in mirror-writing behind their eyes, weigh grains of rice on imaginary scales, picture themselves lying on a bed of red velvet. Most just pop a pill. That has never really worked for me. The tranquilizer would turn things foggy very quickly and for a moment I would feel the world behind my eyelids begin to spin as I sank deeper. But the next instant it would all kick off and I would be swamped by an onslaught of images. At unbridled speed, old fears, old faces, old objects from my past would come charging through my mind. And there I'd be, transfixed all over again by a monstrosity in white plaster, my grandfather's leg, the one they eventually lopped off.

I never encountered Ton. As far as I know, I have never dreamed of him. Or if I did, it must have been when I dreamed I was awake. It happens. I know of people who sleep soundly but dream they have been tossing and turning all night and wake up in the morning exhausted. So it is possible that I have gone downstairs in my dream, turned on the kitchen light, and taken the big bowl and the small bowl down off the shelf. And that, at some point, I recalled the strange, subtle scent that hung in the air at the funeral home.

"Did the corners of his mouth always turn down like that?" I asked Lucia. "Do you know?" And she stepped away from the immaculate vertical pleat of a gray funeral home curtain, looked down beside me and said, "Nah. 'Course not." This triggered thoughts of the note, the farewell letter, the explanation. A few people had asked. I had hunted high and low, but I had yet to find one. As I turned away from my late husband's face, impervious now to tears or laughter, and walked toward the door, it occurred to me for the first time that there was no note. My husband had shaken off his existence, including our time together, without a word. A private matter, that was all it had ever been. He would not permit anyone to read what had held sway over his life, or rather his death, not a single soul. Stepping out into the warm sunshine with Lucia, I felt the need to say something momentous.

"I will never be young again."

"Oh, cut it out," she replied.

I should not be up and about tonight. On a night like this I should be in bed, down for the count, resting soundly against the hipbone of a man. Given half a chance, I try to arrange a firm support for the small of my back. I lie on my side, legs pulled up in front of me, and roll back. And as soon as I feel solid ground behind me, I lean into the bone and feel my spine settle.

Tonight is different. I can't put my finger on what's keeping me awake. Today was pleasant. Everything that happened today was ordinary—ordinary in the most baffling way. I step away from the counter. My breathing is a little heavier now, but I am still not tired. In a few minutes it will be half past two. I wipe my hands and set the kitchen timer. After all my exertions, the dough is ready and now needs an hour to rise. I cover the bowl with a damp dish towel and place it on the little stool beside the radiator. Anatole gets to his feet. His jaws yawn wide and a peep escapes from his throat.

He was all for the idea. Though he did wonder whether the animals would feel like braving the cold. I told him I had heard that lions and tigers don't mind snow in the least. That they even get a kick out of it. But lions and tigers aside, perhaps it would be best to stick to the indoor enclosures on a morning like this? And I told him about the owl cave, the reptile house, and the heated aviary where the rain forest birds were free to flit around.

Though it was only a short walk from the station, we set off at a brisk pace. I left my car parked on a side street. The center of town was busy. The men and women coming toward us looked colorless, the children all seemed to have a cold. Once again, I had a sense of wading against the tide, everyone bent on taking a different path from my own. I knew very well that this was all in my head. Even as a child I had the feeling that most of the other kids were off playing somewhere else.

Today there was someone going my way. Glancing to the side, I saw a look of amusement, cheeks blotched red from the cold. Perfectly at ease with himself, he turned in the direction I pointed out.

We strolled into the bare gardens and there they were, the animals. The white birds of prey. The cattle with their desolate eyes. The wild horses, motionless, waiting. We followed the signs to the aquarium, and distant cries mixed with the scent of the worlds held within the bodies of these exiled creatures lent an air of unreality to our walk.

There was a spring-loaded hinge on the aquarium door. We had to push hard to get in. Bright with curiosity, we walked up the broad marble steps and entered a hall where the walls consisted of tanks teeming with fish. A quiet, twilit place.

"Has it been long?" I asked when we had wandered almost the full length of the hall. In his letter he had written that his wife had left him.

He grasped the thread immediately.

"Over three years," he said. "She left in October."

"What's her name?"

"Louise," he answered.

I knew I could ask any question that entered my head. In these circumstances, there could be no such thing as indiscretion. During one encounter, barely half an hour after laying eyes on the man, I had found myself picking over some peculiar sexual problem or other.

"Is it something you regret?" I asked, for the sake of something to say.

"Regret," he said. "Regret, hmm …"

He seemed to lose himself in thought for a moment. The yellow light from the aquarium made a carnival caricature of his face. I saw that his eyes were following the movement of a flatfish.

Then he said, "When she got out of the bath, her hair curled up like a poodle's. It was all so passionate at the start, a trip through Italy. At night, from our hotel room, you could see a fleet of boats out at sea, four powerful lamps attached to their masts. The fishermen lured their catch to the surface with shafts of light … Look at that!"

I followed his finger. A white shark-like creature had its snout pressed to the glass, gnashing angrily with a mean little mouth.

"It's like the plastic surgeon botched the operation," I said.

"Three or four years in, she was already convinced there was no point staying together when you're no longer in love. But then …"

"But then, there's the children," I hazarded.

He nodded.

"And so we began to make deals."

"Deals …" I echoed.

"Yup. 'A deal's a deal.' That was the deal. You know … so you don't end up waging war over every little thing."

"Ah …"

When we fell silent again, I was suddenly overwhelmed by the stillness of this water palace. I wondered when the other visitors would turn up. The Saturday morning grocery run must be over by now. Or were water and fish the last things people wanted to see on such a cold, cold day?

"One night she chucked a vacuum cleaner at me," he said.

I turned and looked at him, speechless.

"I was just lying there sleeping."

He began to laugh, chuckling silently at first and then out loud, a solid, cheerful laugh. I laughed, too.

"Do you know which ones I like most," he said, turning back to the glass wall. "The plain old codfish."

They were enormous creatures, the slightest sweep of the tail sent them sailing along at high speed. Lips sharply drawn in the dullest of grays, constantly opening and closing. Yes, there was an undeniable beauty in those worried, good-natured faces. Still laughing I said, "I don't believe Ton and I ever got that intense. We simply didn't take the time."

We agreed about us from the very start.

Is that what they call love at first sight? The strange thing was, at the time I never gave it a moment's thought. I couldn't have cared less what it was, why ever since that first day Ton and I simply, unthinkingly, stayed together. There was a casual inevitability to it. Not that I was an ingenue. I knew it could drive you mad. As a child I had devoured enough books to glean a suspicion, and at sixteen I lived through it after my violin teacher ended a lesson by ordering me to sing a pure fifth. To this day, I have never been asked a more intimate question. I gawped at him like a fish, this man with his high forehead and a remarkable light in his eyes. What followed was a rush of afternoons and evenings when I ran through the streets to reach his classroom, at full speed from water's edge to town square. What followed was that I could not see a cloud, a tree, a child without infusing them with elements to which, strictly speaking, they bore no relation whatsoever: his fiery assertion that David Oistrakh was the world's only living musical genius, the scent of cigarettes and lotion that seemed to emanate from behind his hair, the sounds that rose up in him and in me—mysteriously not of our making—when he finally got around to easing me back onto the divan that stood next to the piano. What followed was that I no longer gave a damn about the loneliness that had been handed me at birth. And then, late one glorious day in July, his head and naked shoulders came poking out of the window of his upstairs apartment and he called, "Sorry, you can't come up right now because ... um ... the wisteria has fallen over and jammed the door shut."

With Ton it was different.

It wasn't until my graduation year in Leiden that I fell in with that group of friends. I was practically a teacher already, busy doing school internships on Tuesdays and Thursdays, and flicking through the weekend papers to be reassured that there were plenty of jobs available in elementary schools. It was January, and a protest meeting was being held at the concert hall. Don't ask me what I was doing there. Don't ask me what I was supposed to be up in arms about. I turned up on a whim. And it was on a whim that I left with one of the Neefjes sisters, perched on the back of her bike as she pedaled home to her student quarters on Pietersteeg. A bunch of them lived there: Milou and Dela Neefjes, cheerful girls who both studied math; a pharmacology student called Hugo Kakebeke, who had painted the walls and ceiling of his room midnight blue; and Lucia, who was studying chemistry at the time. No, I didn't meet Ton that evening.

Only Lucia. A farmer's daughter who embraced student life with an allure all her own. That winter, whenever I ran into her in town, she was usually on her way to some urgent gathering or on her way back from one. She was a fixture at all kinds of union committees and action groups, a fervent advocate of the democratization of everything under the sun. But sometimes she would be carrying a tennis racket and a white sports bag. And sometimes she would be wearing brown boots that fitted snugly around the calf and heel. As soon as she saw me she would park her bike. I remember how she would walk next to me, coat always buttoned to the collar, scarf tucked under her chin. All wrapped up like a precious artifact. She was naturally pale and wore her lush red hair long and straight. It was never covered. When she wasn't speaking, she seemed to be in a daydream. When she spoke, she looked straight at you. Light, gray-green eyes. She smiled, was critical yet eager to convince, keen to share her indignation or her delight. To her, sorrow seemed to be an unknown quantity.

Why she took a shine to me, I will never know. But for a girl like me, she was ideal company. I am perfectly willing to come out of my shell; it's just that I have no idea how. During the discussions that filled that first evening, she nudged me several times, smiling at the others, and then back at me. She said things like "Don't you think so too?" and "Yes, I couldn't agree more," and announced to the entire group that she was planning to borrow my sweater sometime.

Less than a week later, Lucia marched into my room one morning, jolting me from a dream of tigers on the prowl. She yanked open the curtains. The statue of the physician Boerhaave that stood outside my window looked greener and colder than ever.

"The Braassem, the Schie, the Wetering are frozen over," she announced. "Even the Singel is all ice. Get up. We're going skating on the canals."

My watch was lying next to the ashtray. Almost ten. I shook my head.

"It's Tuesday. I've got my internship at the Pater

Wijnterp School this afternoon. I've prepared a lesson on the amphibian reproductive system."

She snatched my address book from the table and headed for the door.

"Well, those little brats can kiss their tadpoles goodbye."

As I was pulling on my socks, I heard her dialing a number on the phone out in the hall and then summing up symptoms in a muted, compelling voice. "Swollen glands. A pulsing headache behind the eyes, temples, and forehead."

I hoped she wouldn't overdo it. How was I going to show my face again on Thursday if—

"No," I heard her say. "Thursday's out of the question, too."

We climbed down onto the ice by the derelict paper factory on the Singel. Hugo Kakebeke, the pants of his thick tweed suit tucked into knee-length socks, surprised me by getting off to a sprightly start on his old-school wooden skates. The Neefjes sisters took to the ice like true professionals and—as Lucia and I sat on the embankment fumbling with our laces—they whizzed back and forth in their colorful skating gear, dinky backpacks, knees bent, hips low. Lucia strapped on a backpack, too, provisions for along the way, she explained when I asked. Then she gave me a nudge.

I looked up to see two boys and a girl, none of whom I knew, sliding down the slope of frosted grass to join us. Lucia introduced me to one of the boys, whose every outbreath came as a white cloud. Her brother Ton. I noticed he was wearing her brown-and-white checkered scarf. Hugo Kakebeke yelled to see if we were finally ready to go. I was the last to rise gingerly to my feet. A mist was settling in. Even before we had rounded the bend, ice, air, and quayside had merged into a tunnel of gray.

It's best to focus directly in front of you. By reining in your gaze, you can keep an eye on the color of the ice and the cracks in its surface. Gaze into the distance and you can lose yourself in the primordial trance of the skater: in space, in dreams, in solitude. I heard the calm scrape of skates beside me. No, don't ask if I was curious who was there next to me, riding in a rhythm I could feel from my fingertips down to my toes. Don't ask what we said to each other, in short bursts of conversation to save our breath. Or what it was that made us grind to a halt, unable to contain our laughter, panting, juddering soundlessly side by side. Although neither of us were poor skaters, still we were unable to keep up with the group. By the time we reached the mill at Rijpwetering, an impressive campfire was already crackling away at the bottom of the dike. The rest were huddled around it, Dela and Milou Neefjes dangling tinfoil parcels on sticks into the flames.

"Ton, you are a man who takes milk in his coffee," said Hugo Kakebeke a short while later, proffering a Styrofoam cup. "This I know. Alas, my domestic rigor was not quite up to that this morning."

That winter's day passed without my being able to exert even the slightest influence on events. Ton and I lost sight of the others again when, somewhere close to Hoogmade, the mist thickened for a while. From then on, ditches, fences, and low bridges recurred in such faithful succession that we could do nothing but follow. I experienced a sense of gliding out of the world. There was no wind. No color. No temperature even. Nothing on which to impose my will. Only the sound of the blades on the ice, close beside me.

Dusk had begun to descend when we fell through the ice. We had just agreed to stop at the next village and take the bus back to Leiden when it happened. Sudden as a trapdoor. We shot under a little bridge and all at once there it was, a gleaming black gap in the icy surface. We sank too quickly to scream. I think all I did was sigh.

That night we slept together. How could we not, having survived such a spill?

I can picture us, in my room. On my bed by the window that looked out on the green patina of the statue of Boerhaave, sedentary man of science. It had felt like waking up, Ton and I agreed. No, like being woken. A door thrown open in your face. A jolt to the chest and then an ice-cold flannel …

My memories of that night run deep. The intoxication. The warmth. There was almost no light in my room, but the gas heater burned red and yellow, the glow of stained glass set in solid rock. It was well past midnight. The pleasure of sex still close. Then, as now, I loved the stillness that sinks into my body and my limbs when the heat has burned out and desire takes a pause or simply nods off, a state in which the deepest intimacy can sometimes be reached. We lay stretched on crumpled sheets, my fingertips traced the line of his brow, his nose, his lips and I said, "If I were blind, I would have read your expression now."

We were dead tired. As exhausted as two street bums who, keeping pace with the sinking level in the bottle, have chewed over every detail of what it was to be young and flush before the markets crashed. I believe we tried to get to know each other that night.

He wanted me to know that, although he was studying law, first and foremost he was a farmer's son. That on their farm, flies never buzzed around the kitchen, thanks to the woodwork—painted blue—and the elderberry bush that grew outside the window. That the living room had three tall windows and from November to March you looked out on the bare land and an outbuilding with concrete gutters and stables, vacant but for a single horse. His father was a market gardener, not a livestock farmer. Bedrooms were in short supply. For as long as they lived at home, he and Lucia had slept in two adjacent wooden bunk rooms above the stables. Snug spaces, full of life: their own, the horse beneath them, and the endless flights of hysterically honking geese overhead. Three or four times a year, a storm would pry its way in through the roof and walls, triggering a flurry of repairs.

He wanted me to know that he had lost his mother. That one day he looked at her hands and saw she was no longer wearing her rings. It happened so fast, the wasting away. The aging, too. In the space of three weeks, her hair turned gray. She was thirty-eight. He would come home from school to find her lying in the dark bedroom, enveloped by a strange, sweet smell. Like he said, it all happened so fast. Unbearable, suddenly. Lucia was eleven, he was nearly thirteen. The flowers disappeared from the kitchen garden. His father, sick with grief, remarried that same year, a woman from the village, Mieke Renes, a good-hearted soul who could laugh at nothing and burst into tears for no apparent reason. Salt of the earth, Ton said.

There were other things, too, confidences I no longer recall. One that has stayed with me, as a performance in my mind's eye, is Lucia creeping into his cramped cabin of a bedroom one night to show him how her pet gerbil could crawl up one sleeve of her nightdress and out the other. Later came a tiresome year in which she constantly nagged her brother, insisting they should run away from home together and never come back.

We lay among the pillows at the head of the bed. I

was closest to the window. The props with which the evening had begun lay scattered in the glow of the heater, a smoldering still life on the floor. A couple of glasses, a torn pack of frosted cookies, half-eaten. The cramped shoes from which Ton had freed my feet. To help him remove the pants without ripping them, I had knelt on the bed. It had taken me a while to work out how to unfasten the buckle. Shedding these strange clothes—and I do mean strange—had been a matter of some urgency.

One thing cannot go unremembered: the instant pleasure I felt in making love with him that first night. Perhaps he had told me, between one tale and another, how he had come by that talent, foreshadowed in the solemnity with which he slid the pinching shoes from my feet. Who can say, but thinking back on my own past flings, in him I seemed to have stumbled on a lover with an instinct for reading delicacies and desires in the scent of my skin. Ton certainly didn't fuck like a farm boy.

A little later, I stared out of the window alone. Ton was asleep. Snow began to fall. The snowflakes danced in the beam of the brazen spotlight that kept poor old Boerhaave from his slumbers, and gradually covered the man and his book in a translucent blanket. I was woozy beyond belief, skin glowing as if I had spent a day at the beach. There was an ache behind my eyes.

Who knows how long it throbbed there, but I was suddenly seized by the certainty that every word I had heard and had spoken that evening was a fabrication, plucked from thin air. Dished up for us by the venerable green specter outside my window.

After a while, I turned my head away. How still Ton was as he slept. The heater had gone out. My eyes wandered over the vague contours of a desk, a chair, the vertical metal line of a shelf unit, and failed to make even the slightest connection between them.

The clothes of two strangers were strewn across the floor.

"The clothes of two complete strangers were strewn across the floor," I told him.

He raised a skeptical eyebrow. I had summed up our night as survivors in a string of dry facts. Perhaps he thought I was trying to inject a touch of melodrama.

"No, honestly," I said. "Not a stitch belonged to us."

We sauntered up the ramp that separated the aquarium from the amphibians. Here, too, we found ourselves half in darkness, but a different smell hung in the air, damp and earthy. Pleasant in its way. The trickle of water on all sides.

Somewhere in the distance, deafening screeches erupted. I listened for a while, and then said, "They belonged to a couple of teenagers: corduroy pants, sweaters, underwear. Even the socks and shoes."

"What the hell is that?" he asked.

"Birds of prey. The zookeepers chuck rodents their way at twelve-thirty sharp."

We peered into a display case bathed in grayish light. Clumps of stone. Sand. An overhanging fringe of ferns. At first sight there was nothing else to see in this miniature wilderness. Whatever lived here was hiding from us, or no longer existed and had yet to be replaced.

"You were lucky," he said, without taking his eyes off the glass case. "Someone fished you out. Helped you off the ice."

"No, there wasn't a living soul for miles around. We heaved ourselves out of the water. Scrambled over the rim of cracking ice on our knees and elbows, made it across to the embankment. There was no point even trying to take off our skates. Feet wide apart, we staggered along in our freezing clothes. Scanned our surroundings and spotted a little house along the way. It turned out to be a fashionable bungalow. You know the kind: two Airedale terriers chained up behind the door. But the lady of the house saw immediately what state we were in. She bundled Ton into a hot shower and ran me a bath. The batty old girl sat there the whole time, nattering away. Showed us photos of her kids. Perhaps she was just glad of a chance to talk about them. Son and daughter, both at boarding school in Switzerland. Busy growing out of their clothes."

He pointed. "Hah! There they are."

Even so, it took me a while to spot them. They had been right under our noses all this time, rendered invisible by lack of motion. A pair of toads, big as fists. Dull gray, like something an old miner might cough up.

Next to every terrarium was a picture accompanied by an informative text. Out of habit, I absorbed a few factoids. Perhaps I already had an inkling about what tree frogs have to do to find themselves a mate. The males emit cries while the picky females listen intently. Set on breeding success, they will settle for nothing less than a male whose call vibrates at an exact frequency, thirty trills per second for example, which equates to a body temperature of 61 degrees. That's how a female tree frog knows she has found herself a reliable specimen. The precision of all this appealed to me. Is it so strange that, now and then, I have found myself wondering exactly what prompted me to accept Ton as the love of my life without a second thought?

Just as we were about to head out into the cold again, the door was thrust open and we had to take a hurried step back. Two elderly women in wheelchairs were pushed in, one after the other. Despite the verve of the two young girls at the helm, the second chair caught on the threshold. One of the old women, sporting an orange rabbit-skin coat, gazed up at me goggle-eyed, brandished a baked roll, and said, "Sausage on white bread ... You can't beat it!" What came over me I do not know, but as we passed the jackals on the way to the restaurant, I was struck by an image of myself as a girl of eight or nine, scooping a hollow in the soil under the pine trees so that I could play marbles. The ground was hard. You had to cup your fingers and hold them steady, the dirt worked itself all the way under your fingernails, and when you finally came home in the dark, runny-nosed and numb with cold, the table was set for dinner and the lamp shining down on the white tablecloth almost hurt your eyes.

Settling down at our table in the restaurant, we talked about the past, about home, and we each wanted to know what the other had missed out on most. The food had yet to arrive, but a bottle of wine had been uncorked and stood on a silver-plated tray. He filled a glass, held it out to me, and I said without the slightest hesitation, "Belonging." And he, one of seven children as it turned out, said, "Privacy."

The night is at its coldest now. I do not need a clock to tell me how deep the darkness is. I can hear it in the cold. The timer has just called me back to the kitchen but I am in no rush. Haste will not help this job along. I press my forehead to the windowpane, feel and hear the cold beyond the glass. It comes in the distant howl of a dog, in the hiss of a passing train, its vibration concentrated, polished by the cold. It comes in the crack of branches encased in ice. I stand barefoot on a coconut-fiber mat. To my left and my right lies the land that is mine by law.

Behind me, Anatole snorts and starts gnawing at his crotch. What am I to make of all this?

"Nothing," I murmur and write the word on the fogged-up glass with my finger.

Then I take the large mixing bowl from the little stool and lift the dish towel. The mixture has risen to the brim. With a nod of satisfaction, I use two spoons to transfer it to the Bundt pan and, as I do this, I won-der—not for the first time—if there is anyone who can explain it to me.

Perhaps I could have laid it out for him, this afternoon?

The fact that I lived so agreeably with my hus-band, on the very best of terms—we both thought that there was nothing better than sleeping between starched white sheets, that it made sense to do the gro-cery run once a month on a Wednesday afternoon, when hordes of housewives were otherwise occupied, that the postman was the spitting image of the care-taker at the teacher training college, that the sloping bosom of the woman next door made her look like a seagull, that we would wait another three years before having children—convinced life's great passions still lay ahead of us. And yes, those passions showed up soon enough, and fell on fallow ground. The love, the hatred, the fascination with everything he had or had not done, fascination that spiraled into fervid curiosity. Into obsession. Into madness.

After lunch, I suggested we take a walk in the ice forest.

"The ice forest?" he repeated, as he struggled into his coat.

I explained that the forests here in the North were frozen. Before it could drip from the branches, the meltwater turned to ice. The trees were enveloped in transparent sheaths, a very sad, very beautiful sight. The slightest touch, by man or bird, caused the wood to snap.

As we stepped out onto the pavement, we noticed that the sun was on the verge of breaking through the clouds. The sky was milky blue. I drove us out of town. Forced to keep my eyes on the road, I made a few routine inquiries.

"What age are your children?"

"Eighteen and sixteen."

"Do you see them often?"

He did not answer straight away, but began running his fingers along the edge of the floor.

"The handle is under the seat, on the right," I said.

The seat slid back and he stretched his legs.

"The police came knocking," he said and told me that his sons belonged to a group of boys who had managed to hack into the computer systems of an unlikely assortment of institutions. Not a shred of data was beyond their reach. His teenage sons were walking around with payroll lists, medical records, and the names of debt defaulters and investment fraudsters in their back pockets. Just for laughs.

This tickled me and made me think of what he had said about his own work that morning.

"So they take after their dad."

"How come?"

"Facts, facts ..." I began to say but clamped my lips together as I felt the wheels begin to slide. I eased up on the gas, let the car right itself, and, once I was back in control, steered it toward the center of the road.

He seemed oblivious to my maneuvers.

"There's something wild and angular about the way they move. Like a pair of young colts," he said. "They take after Louise."

Louise. This was the second mention of her name. I felt I was getting to know her rather well. A woman with a tangle of damp curls and a knot of anger in her belly. She had brought two sons into the world. Her lovemaking was angular and wild. Her husband had loved her deeply.

Fleeting confidences. Free, no strings attached. Steering and switching gears on this freezing afternoon, I could have added up the exact balance of my life with ease, like a sum scribbled on the back of an envelope. An unremarkable man, the man who had shared less than eighteen months of my life, had—after a shooting incident in a darkened greenhouse— become a secret that would drive me to distraction.

After that first, fateful day, we saw each other three or four times a week, mostly in the company of others. That winter was a season of unrest in every university town: riots broke out, fires were started, a barricade could spring up on any street corner within thirty minutes. The group to which Lucia and Ton belonged was intensely involved in all this, but then so was the student population as a whole. Even I found myself prying cobbles from the street, screaming bitter slogans, and spitting at the barred windows of a dark-blue police van packed with vigilant energy.

One thing that has stayed with me is the constant warmth that radiated toward Ton and me. Everyone seemed delighted that the two of us were an item. Congratulations and invitations were the order of the day. What are you two drinking? And before we could so much as blink, we'd be standing there, beer in hand.

Easter arrived and we all went sailing on the Kaag. Blustery conditions had been keeping everyone on their toes all week, but on the day we decided to join in the fun, the wind died down and by the afternoon the entire fleet of rainbow yachts, two of which we crewed, resembled a cloud bank dissipating at a barely perceptible pace. Hugo Kakebeke, whose black humor I had come to know and appreciate, lazed by the rudder surveying us all in turn. "Ton," he declared, "I see baldness and corpulence in your future." About me he said nothing.

One Sunday we paid his father and his stepmother a visit. We took the train and then the bus and arrived in a village that consisted of farmhouses and a single convenience store. Dogs scampered around off the leash, roosters crowed, and goats grazed in front gardens. Everyone we encountered said hello.

In the kitchen with the blue paintwork, we were welcomed by Mieke Renes. She took both my hands in hers and squeezed them tightly. Suddenly her eyes grew red and tears began to roll down her cheeks.

"Your father is out on the land," she said to Ton, as she turned away and went in search of the cat. She was a woman of around fifty, sturdily built. A hand-knitted cardigan drooping to one side accentuated the round-ing of her shoulders. As we walked in the sunshine to the greenhouse where the chicory was grown, Ton told me his stepmother had been a spinster who, until the age of forty, had looked after her father, a schoolmas-ter forced into retirement by illness and demanding beyond belief. When she married Ton's father, she had abruptly left her old man to the tender mercies of the district nurse.

Ton's father had only recently embarked on this horticultural experiment and he was brimming over with enthusiasm. He showed us the water system, the darkness behind the rubber curtain, and the cold store where the roots lay in the misapprehension that it was winter. At dinner, Ton and his father could scarcely speak of anything else. Later, as we washed the dishes, Mieke Renes and I watched them head out into the fields together, two farmers in overalls, crotches half-way to their knees. "Ton is getting more and more like his father," said Mieke Renes and I was left wonder-ing why this statement was accompanied by a peal of laughter.

In no time at all, the pieces of my life fell clatter-ing into place. In May, I graduated. One week later,

I slipped two job application letters in the mailbox and headed over to Pietersteeg where everyone was in shock. Lucia and Ton had left only fifteen minutes earlier, I was told. Devastating news. Their father had suffered a heart attack that day. Yes, he was dead. Dressed in gray, I sat beside Ton at the funeral. The service was accompanied by the loud sobbing of Mieke Renes, until the moment when she jumped up and stormed out of the church—I can still picture her, running with knees lifted high, the way children run. That same day she let everyone know she was moving back in with her father. Ton and Lucia spent a week talking things over with the notary and the bank. They examined the books. It was June. The countryside was bathed in glorious sunshine and the night rains smelled of grass. The farm badly needed taking care of and Ton decided to stay on and leave Leiden behind. We married in early July and fourteen months later I was a widow.

That was that.

"Light me a cigarette, would you?" I said.

There was more, of course, but that was another chapter.

Trees suspended in ice rolled by on either side. They looked like some exotic species. The branches hung unnaturally low, some of the treetops were crooked, not dangerously so, but still: a slight distortion and the familiar becomes strange enough to inspire fear or awe.

I stopped at a parking lot dotted with trash cans and signs bearing directions for walking trails. Before we got out of the car, he slotted a cigarette between my lips. The insides of his fingers felt rough.

I may be mistaken—it's late, the middle of the night, and I am standing over a Bundt pan smoothing out cake batter—but I seem to remember him looking intently at my face. Perhaps he was toying with the idea of asking "And then?"

Had he asked, I would have answered, "And then began my search, my descent into madness."

But he didn't ask anything.

It was spring before it occurred to me to retrace his movements.

One morning I found myself standing in front of the wardrobe, staring for minutes on end, as if there were some need to be watchful. The wardrobe was a hulking great thing made of walnut, with two small mirrors set in the upper panels of the doors at a height that made no human sense. Overcoming indecision, I swung the doors wide. All our clothes were hanging there. Ton's to the right. A few coats, a few jackets, shirts and sweaters. I was looking for my blue linen skirt. There was a March chill in the air, but I knew sunlight would soon be pouring in through the windows of my classroom. The peacoat Ton had worn that winter in Leiden caught my eye. Without thinking, I ran my hand over the indestructible fabric, unfastened a button, and felt the lining, still remarkably soft and luxurious to the touch. A coat made for a high-ranking officer. Then my fingers slid into the inside pocket and fished out a long ticket.

It was the punch card for a parking garage in Leiden.

"Thursday, March second, nineteen-seventy," I read aloud. "Two thirty p.m."

Over two years ago. I counted back. We had only just met.

Contrary to habit, I did not take the car to school that morning. My farmhouse is a short walk from the village, ten minutes at most, but the lightest shower is enough to flood the road under the viaduct, and the embankments I have to step onto when cars come up behind me are soft and muddy. That day I felt like walking. I played with the punch card in my coat pocket, nodded to the drivers who had to slow down behind me, and reached the village just as the storekeeper was putting out his sign announcing the week's special offers. I bought a newspaper and began to chat about the weather.

They don't understand me around here. Since that September day, they haven't noticed much of a change. My beautiful hair has not fallen out. My hands are no thinner, nor are they stained brown with nicotine. That Christmas Lucia and Hugo Kakebeke came to call and everyone saw us striking off across the fields in the highest of spirits in our shabby old fur coats, with Anatole trailing along behind us. Only a pup back then, he had misjudged the distance, covered it twice, and then had to drag himself over the final leg, hunched low on his paws.

Worst of all, of course, is the fact that I did not leave. I can't say I understand it myself. I could have gone back to my own village, by the sea. My mother would have let me sleep late in the mornings, she would have bought new T-shirts for me—just my size—and when a little time had passed I could have looked out of my new classroom window to see gulls squabbling in the schoolyard. But that was impossible. There was something here that still had to be unearthed, though I had no idea what. Until that morning I had taken things easy. Until that morning I had a sense that as long as I did not disturb anything, spoil anything, I had an eternity ahead of me …

By ten thirty my classroom was bathed in sunlight. I strode past the rows of desks, shoes creaking, and tested the children on their geography homework.

"How deep is the Pacific Ocean?" I asked a little blond thing.

She looked at me gravely and thought a moment.

"A million fathoms."

"How cold is the North Pole?" I asked the boy sitting next to her.

He lowered his eyes.

"Hundred degrees below zero," he whispered.

I prodded the girl in the back row gently to wake her up.

"If you lay all the roads on planet earth end to end, how many miles would they stretch?"

She, too, took the question seriously.

"A hundred thousand," she said calmly.

The class sat there looking up at me, helpful and attentive. I haven't the faintest idea why I got it into my head to ask them these idiotic questions. Perhaps I wanted to see whether they would laugh at me. Perhaps I was begging these children for understanding and tolerance that might extend to the other bizarre questions that were tumbling harum-scarum though my mind. They like me. They think I am pretty. Today of all days, in my blue outfit, they think I am pretty. Strolling past the desks I had felt a small hand brush my angora cardigan once or twice.

"Put away your books," I said. "I want you to draw me a lovely picture of some cows."

I walked back to my desk and sat down. Chin resting on my knuckles, I stared down at the item of evidence propped up against the vase of flowers. On Thursday, March 2, 1970, I had been teaching at Pater Wijnterp Elementary School. That same afternoon, at two thirty, Ton had been behind the wheel of a car, pulling into one of those newfangled, automated garages.

Something had begun. Behind my eyes, a tiny mechanism had been set in motion. The whirring, though not unpleasant, ran on steadily and left me distracted. On several occasions, I walked out of the convenience store without so much as a goodbye. Silly mistakes in the children's notebooks went uncorrected. I still had no trouble falling asleep, but for weeks I'd had no need of an alarm clock. With a jolt born of gnawing restlessness, I would wake at the first light of dawn and, thoughts from the night before still fully formed, I would get up and go downstairs.

I had collected my finds and laid them out in the living room. The contents of the drawers now covered the desk. The long dining table, one of the few pieces of his parents' furniture Ton had wanted to keep after our marriage, was strewn with movie tickets, sales receipts, coins, buttons, pieces of string, his pocket diary: all items I had dug out by rifling through his pockets and a couple of bags. On the floor stood a box of family photos and documents, a modest collection, since Ton had sorted everything after the death of his father.

As soon as I entered the room, the restlessness subsided. My material was laid out before me, entirely at my disposal, nothing had been snatched away in the night. Secure in this knowledge, I was able to get dressed and put on the kettle. And then with a guilty glow, full of tenderness and love for the foolish creature, I could throw open the door and join Anatole on a ramble across the sodden field.

A few hours later, there I'd be, sipping coffee with a couple of colleagues. Half an ear tuned to the tenor of the cries from the schoolyard, we would chat about some TV show and meantime I would be trying to recall if I had turned over a particular photograph—the schoolboy in what looked like a new suit, arms stiffly at his sides—in case a date might be scrawled on the back. And it felt like I was being held in check. Impatience sent the blood rising to my cheeks.

To begin with, Lucia was little use to me. She came over a couple of times a week, hearty and cynical as ever. We cooked dinner together and talked. She offered to give me horse-riding lessons, insisting that her mare was the most docile animal you could imagine. The summer of my wedding, Lucia had also returned to the North, using her part of the inheritance to purchase a disused property on a secluded stretch of land. Her horse was first to make the move. After a dogged renovation, much of it carried out with her own hands, Lucia followed, and had taught at the riding school ever since. She saw no point in my detective work. For a while, I suspected her of blunt insensitivity.

"When was this?" I asked her.

She was sitting on the floor inspecting Anatole's teeth and looked up reluctantly at the color photograph I was holding, an outdoor scene snapped from the farmhouse one summer's day. A collection of children and adults out on the lawn, sitting around a table in the sunshine, framed by the dark stable doors. All posing for the camera, except for one little girl who could not contain her laughter. Swallowed by the light, smiling, glass in hand, these people had consented to halt the course of their lives for a moment.

"How should I know?" she said and peered closely at the dog's coat. "He's got a tick." She crooked her thumb and index finger and they disappeared among the hair.

His father I recognized. The woman leaning back without a care in the world was probably his mother. Then there were uncles, aunts, two plump cousins. Ton was a schoolboy in short pants and sandals. Curls tamed in a side part, eyebrows bleached by the sun. Lucia was leaning into him, trying to suppress a burst of laughter with outstretched fingers while keeping her eyes on the lens.

"Why were you laughing so much?"

She shot me a testy look.

The day came when I asked her point-blank. "Why did he do it?"

I screamed it at her over the din of a paint sprayer. Lucia had lined the walls of her attic with fiberboard tiles and was giving them a coat of whitewash. I had been helping out where I could, impressed by her strength and precision. She wielded the high-pressure contraption like a weapon. Hitting the off button, she half-turned away from me, put the sprayer down, and kicked it hard. My own anger flared in a heart-beat, had perhaps been building for some time. I circled her in two brisk steps, determined to look her in the face. At first, she avoided my stare. Then she met it full on. What reality had we crossed into? For a moment we stood opposite each other, raw with anger. Fists clenched, grimacing with pain, helpless rivals who knew each other through and through in their fight for the same man.

The intolerable moment passed. It passed with our mutual consent. What were we supposed to do with it? Surrounded by the beat of the flapping plastic that still covered the front of the house, the sound of the wind, wood freshly sawn, whitewash, the sound of here and now, the lack of understanding, the unfathomable lack of understanding between Lucia and me.

"He just did," she said, with our mutual consent.

As we left the house, she told me she had seen the pistol once, as a little girl. Their father had laid the weapon down on the living room table, wrapped in a clean white diaper from the layette purchased when either she or Ton was born. In the lamplight, he unfolded the cloth. She looked on, reached out and touched the metal briefly. She remembered thinking how much fun it would be, how easy, to curl her finger round the trigger and squeeze. But then, she had been only nine years old.

One evening in June, Lucia and I were sitting out back, talking under the overhang by the kitchen. A mild rain fell. Wine cooler within reach, one of my—no longer our—wedding gifts. A bottle of Pouilly to mark my birthday. Lucia flicked the butt of her cigarette into the damp dusk and began reminiscing about her brother's hitchhiking vacation. She, seventeen at the time and envious of his freedom, had wanted to know every detail when he got back home. Ton and the girl had managed to hitch a ride in a sports car that had taken them all the way to a village west of Paris in a single trip. They had slept in the open field, amid Van Gogh landscapes. The girl had a habit

of laughing in her sleep. They spent a week in Valmondois, where a tottering old priest had given them
lodging in a room that was swathed in red velvet: the
chairs, the bedspread, even the walls up to shoulder
height. Ton dubbed it the Bishop's Suite. There was a
river nearby where, with a bit of luck, you could catch
fish with your bare hands. On Sunday, their host said
Mass in a neighboring hamlet where, apart from a
frail old lady who declaimed the tale of *Poil de carotte*
all through the liturgy, they were the only worshippers.

"Butry," I said.

She turned to face me and, in the light of the outdoor lantern, I saw her features twist into an expression
I had never seen before.

"What?"

"That was in Butry," I exclaimed and dashed into
the house.

The diary was exactly where I had left it. I knew
there was nothing more to prove by flicking through
the pages, but I wanted to see the notes with my own
eyes. There! There they were! Why hadn't Lucia come
to see? Look, here it is, written in ballpoint. Friday,
August 2nd: *arrived in Paris, on to Auvers.* Tuesday, the
5th: *Valmondois, beautiful weather, 78°, grand bed in Bishop's
Suite.* Then Sunday, the 10th: *Butry, farewells, heading south* … I heaved a deep sigh. These things had
actually happened. Tonight, all these facts had been

filled with life: with sleeping laughter, with a deep-blue starry night, a room of red velvet, flailing fish, with a childlike creature who knew her classics … The stuff of real life, from this moment on.

I put the diary back in its place, among the other exhibits.

Since my absence had become too much for her, my mother pulled into the driveway unannounced one midsummer morning to entice me back home for a week or two. She had redecorated my room, she said, and hung my favorite painting on the wall. I know her well and almost instantly hit upon a stratagem to resist my evacuation. My dear mother is a talker and a woman who likes to get things done. And so, in high spirits and chatting all the while, we began to check off the chores that had been staring me in the face for months. She left as evening fell, more or less reassured. I walked her out to her car, kissed her fondly, and closed the car door as she started the engine. She immediately rolled down the window so that she could wave goodnight. I watched from the path as the maternal arm disappeared into the darkness of the road.

In the freshly scrubbed house, I returned to my post at the desk. As I rubbed my fingertips back and forth across my forehead, I felt the strangeness of the day ebb away behind my eyes. The whirring in my head, and its unlikely hint of happiness, began to carry me off again.

As they so often did, the hours evaporated without my noticing. I got up once to brew a pot of coffee and look for my smokes, and out of nowhere the clock struck midnight. By this stage, I had become intimately acquainted with the contents of the desk drawers. Roughly speaking, the items fell into one of two categories. The notes, stencils, and syllabi of a degree in law, and a discursive analysis of the latest methods in greenhouse horticulture. All the evidence on both sides spoke of someone who had been hard at work with complete conviction. When we met, Ton had been on the brink of graduating in law; five months later, he was a farmer. A little queasy from coffee and smoke, I considered the fact that my husband had been a man capable of decanting his passions from one vessel to another without the least hesitation.

During these months, I was not troubled by the thought that everything I stumbled across was entirely his business. His textbooks. His farmer's overalls and clogs. His house that, despite the renovation we had plunged into with typical newlywed enthusiasm, had remained his parental home, complete with the two childhood bunk rooms under the stable roof. It was among these things that his secret lay, not with me. To my surprise, the top shelf of the bookcase turned out to be full of books on polar expeditions, north and south. I had never even known it was an interest of his.

But there came a day when, hands trembling with rage, I grabbed the still life on the bathroom shelf and flung it away. Shaving brush, shaving soap, razor: objects that knew more of him than I did. It was maddening, sickening. With every step of my investigations, he seemed to withdraw further into himself, to grow colder, lonelier.

I redoubled my efforts. At night I got up to listen to his music. He had been a jazz lover, the big bands especially. Basie, Ellington. At full blast, *The Individualism of Gil Evans* burrowed its way into my head. Sounds he had heard.

Early one afternoon, as the rain hammered down, I installed myself at the arched window in the stable—surely a boyhood hideaway of his—only to jerk awake to the sound of my own murmuring. Somewhere a clock struck five, from all sides came the urgent lowing of cattle, there was a smell of burned leaves and, gazing out as he must have done, I saw open skies, where the rain had given way to a light reflecting so brightly that I did not know where to look.

I got up as fast as I could, determined to pour myself a stiff brandy and knock it back in one gulp. In my haste, I yanked open both doors of the kitchen dresser recently tidied up by my mother. Arms spread wide, I scanned the shelves. Where was the bottle? My gaze skimmed neat rows of pots and preserving jars and lit upon three labels written in a faded motherly hand. I picked one out. *Brandied raisins*. *September*. Then came a date that had become illegible in the course of what must have been a dozen years or so.

I slurped down the raisins and drained the liquid. Three jars of soaked fruit and old brandy disappeared inside me and stirred up a glow of gratitude. Overjoyed, I sat there at the kitchen table. Night fell. I did not move. Even the empty jars and sticky spoon failed to spur me to action. I reveled in my drowsiness. I grinned at my clarity.

"If you want to know who your husband was," an unassuming inner voice suggested, "it might not be a bad idea to find someone who can tell you a thing or two about his mother."

I waited on the doorstep. The echo in the house died away. Hands thrust in my coat pockets, I looked at the house number and the glossy coat of Brunswick green staring me in the face. You could wait a long time at this door, I sensed. As if something inside had to be hidden away first.

At last she appeared on the threshold. Mieke Renes. Smiling, arms outstretched.

"You of all people!" she cried. "Believe it or not, you've been on my mind for quite a while."

Once she had ushered me into the living room, she bustled into the kitchen to make tea. She left the doors open and bridged the distance by firing off the kind of questions that barely call for an answer. How are you doing? How's your new class?

"Oh yes," she said a little later, as we sat facing each other. "I knew his mother her whole life long."

I didn't have to do another thing, not so much as raise a finger. No need to liven things up with a question or a smile. Mieke Renes was able to give her memories free rein, since Ton's mother's life had for a large part been her own. Her village, her school. Her unspoken, unrequited love.

And so I wasn't always able to tell exactly which of the girls had long brown hair, which of them in 1930 thought it was an unbelievable adventure to write in ink, who knew exactly when and how deep to plant seeds in the soil, who would burst into uncontrollable fits of laughter or could launch into an anecdote at the drop of a hat, and who had been in love with a strapping young farmer.

Not that it mattered much. After a while, it mattered so little that I didn't even try to keep track: the Depression years, the war, the two lovers who married shortly after Liberation Day. Whatever she said, every word circled around Ton.

Eventually, she interrupted herself.

"Now then, what can I fix you to drink?"

Her face flushed and happy, she pulled the cork

from a bottle of port, aged for thirty years. I eyed the glass warily, the ghost of the brandied raisins not yet put to rest.

Just as we had raised our glasses, a couple of loud thumps sounded through the wall.

"What was that?" I asked, and in the same moment I realized that her bedridden father must still be somewhere in the house. In the village I'd heard talk that he wasn't long for this world, a few more weeks at most.

"Three knocks," Mieke Renes said impassively. "He'll be wanting his dram."

But she remained seated and picked up her story where she had left off, with Ton's outpouring of grief after the death of his mother. I nipped at my port, already feeling the effects. I had no objection to getting drunk again, but I had hopes of pacing myself this time. "Sure," I thought calmly. "Tell me about it, death and the havoc it wreaks."

Looking to the side, I could see through the bay window and out into the street beyond. The narrow sidewalks. The women with their shopping bags. Saturday. In front of a shop sign, a poplar tree was swaying in the wind. I felt a fondness for it somehow, a riddle I recognized but would never be able to solve …

"Well, what do *you* think?" Mieke Renes exclaimed.

Obediently, I turned back to her.

"I accepted his proposal in a flash! Fine, I told him, just let me know when."

She refilled our glasses, her tongue pressed between her teeth, and what a spell she cast over me now, Mieke Renes and her life story. The tale of a woman who, at forty, had a happiness she never counted on land in her lap, who for almost ten years had felt pretty much at home in that happiness, and who, when that happiness died, returned to the life she had known since girlhood, a life she perhaps thought suited her better.

Her voice had taken on a tone of surprise and of tenderness. She gave me the lowdown on Ton.

"… can't say I ever remember him being reluctant to do his bit. Off he'd trot to the village or out onto the moor to gather moss for the Christmas manger. I could ask him to do anything. When he set off for school, he made a point of cycling past the kitchen,"—she craned her neck and took such a lively look over my head that I almost turned to see who was passing—"to give me one last wave. Of course, in my heart I always knew it was just his way, something he used to do when his mother was still alive, something he wanted to hold on to."

She was quiet for a moment and then she said, "Sometimes, when I was standing at the stove, I had to be careful not to step on the toes of that wise and caring phantom who stood right behind me, helping me stir the soup."

The loud noise came again. The sound of a stick pounding on the floor. I counted.

"Four knocks," I said.

She nodded.

"Yes. Four. That means he wants me to plump his pillows so he can sit up and wave to Braams. He always comes by on his tractor around five, and turns on his flashing blue light by way of a greeting. My father likes to wave back."

And she began to speak about the family life in which she had shared as a stepmother. Four years, five at most, until Ton and Lucia moved out and into their student digs. Even so, there were all those Sunday visits to enjoy, the pies, puddings, and pans brimming with food. The winter breaks, with skating, boots under the coat stand, and clotheslines strung across the attic where, when it rained, the smell of teenage laundry would hang in the air. Oh, and the weeks when Ton and Lucia came home to cram for their assignments and exams! My, those two could be grouchy, you bet your life they could, even with each other. But they never fought. Never. Except for that one time, she had never known things between Ton and his younger sister to turn nasty.

Now we were getting somewhere.

"That one time?"

"Yes. When that boy came over to invite Lucia to

the polo party at the Technical College."

"Polo party? What's that?"

"Oh, some shindig for horsey students."

She had been doing the ironing in the living room, had watched from behind the ironing board, witnessed the pain and the danger without being able to intervene. Lucia and the boy were sitting opposite each other at the end of the long dining table when Ton, working on an assignment at the other end of the table, without getting up, just sitting there in his chair, sent one dart after another whizzing through the air between them. There was a dartboard on the wall at the end of the table, a good twenty feet from Ton, but close to where the other two were sitting.

Mieke Renes gave me a searching look.

"You know the game?"

"Darts? Yes," I said.

He had taken his time over every throw. The sharp, winged projectile poised in his hand for what seemed like an age as he rocked his lower arm back and forth, back and forth … Narrowing his eyes for focus, the way darts players do.

All the while, Lucia and the boy had tried to keep on talking. Lucia remained as cool as ever, but the boy turned white as a sheet. A few of the darts shot right past his nose before slamming into the board on the wall. Yet the boy carried on sitting there, hands out-stretched on the table. It almost looked like he was begging.

"So—do you want to come?" he asked.

She pulled a face that hinted she was weighing the offer seriously, drawing out her decision. And— wham!— another dart came hurtling between them at eye level and drilled into the bulls-eye at the heart of the board.

"Oh!" I gasped.

"Yes," Mieke Renes answered.

"And what about the look on Ton's face?"

"Funny you should ask ... To be honest, he looked exactly like his sister. The pair of them seemed to be completely in tune while that horrible scene played out. Only difference was that he, Ton I mean, looked tense. Only logical, I suppose. A blue vein was pulsing just above his temple. His back arched slightly. And that's when he would throw, straight as an arrow."

Mieke Renes and I looked at each other. I watched as her face, tight with unexplained fascination, began to soften. In the telling, her impression had changed, too.

"Oh, what a lousy thing for Lucia to go through."

"I'll say!" I exclaimed. "Downright mean!"

I stared down at my feet on the floral carpet. Bully. Jerk. Sneak. Asshole. Uptight bitch. Exotic words, insults we never exchanged. Never a slammed door or a car screeching out of the driveway, no floods of silent tears between the sheets. We never had time to get around to these things.

The growl of an engine approaching. I felt the floor begin to vibrate.

"Hey," it occurred to me to ask. "Did Lucia end up going to that party?"

"Yes, I believe she did."

Braams's tractor came thundering past the house. A sudden swirl of blue light gave Mieke Renes the face of a sorceress. A sorceress who burst into tears.

I pace the perimeter of my living room in the dark and it pleases me to do so. The Russian Bundt cake needs at least another hour and a quarter of heat from the oven. I could just as easily turn on the light and devote this time to some chore or other. As they pass, the hours bring none of the calm I know so well from other nights of sleepwalking. I hear a succession of short, sharp cracks, which tells me that the wood of one of the ash trees over by the chicory greenhouse is splitting. All night the trees have been exposed to the east wind, its hostile breath well below freezing. Now, at the brink of dawn, it is more than their trunks can take and cracks begin to sound. Each time this happens, I see Anatole's glassy eyes shining up at me. I know that he knows where my instinct is leading me.

Given the choice, I would rather dwell on what awaits me in ninety minutes or so, two hours at most: the prospect of easing my body into a heavy, drowsy warmth that—I'll admit it, regardless of who is in my bed—leaves me feeling satisfied, deeply satisfied, time after time. Tonight, there's an additional charge of pleasure building inside me, fueled by the pleasure of the afternoon.

Who would have thought I would find myself walking with a total stranger through a frozen forest ever again, without the need to say anything much at all? Convinced we are both seeing the same things? A strip of smoldering red above the trees to the west. Close by, a beech that ripped up a patch of the ice floor when it fell. To see such things and let them pass in silence. No knee-jerk responses to a crash in the fog, the snap of something breaking, splitting, falling, no trotting out things they remind you of, simply because you've had a few other notable experiences in your life. Wasn't this the kind of silence that existed between old friends?

Since the night still has a ways to go and I am beginning to feel the cold, I step into the hallway and take the brown coat from the stand. I put it on. It is heavy and hangs almost to my feet. Men's coats always smell more strongly of the man than women's coats do of the woman. I find myself wanting one of his cigarettes. His pack lies abandoned on the table, among our plates and glasses. Wrapped in smoke and warmth, I pass the mirror again and turn up the collar of his coat, gazing into my eyes as my face falls away.

"Let's head back," I suggested before we reached the edge of the forest, knowing that the wretched view of the Oostink fertilizer silos was all that lay in wait farther on. And so, we began talking again, this time about the sea. People who have grown up by the sea often share the same memories.

I enjoyed drawing out his recollections. The movement of his hands as he spoke described the scope and the speed of things. The path began to narrow and I ended up walking a few paces ahead. One ear turned back toward him, I carried on listening. A man hunched in a lopsided coat was relaying my own memories back to me. An effortless exchange.

"And in the winter?" I asked.

"Waves crashing over the boulevard above the beach. Lying in bed, weighing up your options. Planning what to take with you if the water rolled into the street. Up onto the roof first, then onto the raft."

"Easter?"

"Traffic jams. Sun beating down on car roofs.

A mountain of stripped hyacinth buds in the back garden."

"Summer?"

He was quiet for a moment. Long enough to let me know he was tiring of this game.

And then he said "Once every summer, a little brother or some other kid you were supposed to look after would get lost on the beach."

"Yes!" I interjected. "And you'd come home exhausted from searching and the little tyke would already be at the table stuffing his face!"

He shook his head. Again I thought, he's had enough.

"Not always," he said and began to talk about searching for hours. How the sand makes everything sluggish and strange. The sea, too, turns slower, stranger. Not the surf, he said, but the gentle motion farther out. The striped tents, the flags, the vacation-blue sky, they all seemed to change. To become unrecognizable. You have crossed into the scene of a disaster. And even so, you do not want to leave. The last thing you want is to leave.

When I glanced back to read his expression, he flashed a smile.

"Can you picture it?" he asked.

It was a time to be alone. Being with other people only wore me out. Idle chatter, social niceties, picking out clothes, applying makeup, I let it all slide. It was only in the classroom that I felt at ease. Sunbeams on my desk and hands. The children, daydreaming, the odd one nodding off from time to time, the rest listening intently to my crisp, lively account of the moors and how small blue flames could shoot out of the peaty ground at night.

In May, I decided to clean the house from top to bottom. That was in the second year, a time when I began to wonder whether, after someone's death, you were entitled to stake a claim to that little piece of territory that, out of nonchalance or sleight of hand, had been kept off limits. After all, I had only been his wife for fourteen months.

I also began to curse my memory. Even with my eyes shut tight it salvaged next to nothing. Nothing of the intimacy I felt sure must have existed, having lived as man and wife for a full fourteen months.

Or ...?

I had thrown out his clothes. Consigned the photos and documents to the attic. Locked up the chicory greenhouse. But my thoughts would not be thwarted. At the oddest moments they set to work, with the monstrous diligence of ants transporting a chunk of wasp or a length of straw to their secret lair.

So there I was, in the merry month of May, sliding upturned chairs onto the table. Heaving the bed and the closets to one side. Vacuuming, mopping the floors. I scoured doorposts, wiped down windowpanes with methylated spirits, and sloshed a pail of soapy water over the floor tiles in the hall. Anyone looking on would have sworn I was intent on wiping out my husband's every last fingerprint, his every footstep.

The opposite was true. Clean a place up and something is sure to surface. As I dragged the kitchen table away from the wall, a stack of cookbooks toppled to the floor, and a handwritten note torn from a diary slipped from between the pages. I picked it up and sat down to read. On June 12, 1971, I had left my husband this note, told him I was sorry but I couldn't wait till he got back from the auction, my mother was expecting me for dinner and I had to allow three hours for the trip. I reminded him to give the rabbits their medication and let him know I would be back before dark the next day. Beneath this I wrote "I love you" and signed my name with a swirly capital.

There could be no doubt.

I had loved my husband. Told you so. There it was. Signed, dated, written in my own hand. I gave a deep sigh and took my place among the exhibits.

The intimacy in the blending of our lives. Something slow began to well up inside me, to pound against the underside of my thoughts. Something real, something true. Dig in a little longer and I would know what it was.

A dress.

It came as a shock. A flood of green, taffeta, long since out of fashion, and here, now, before my eyes. In the same instant I recalled the stiffness of the buttons, made of green taffeta, too, and tricky to fasten. Then came a sky, heavy with an oncoming storm. And there was the question of whether I still felt like going out ...

Peering at the torn page in my hand, I climbed the

stairs. Slowly. My free hand on the bannister, pulling me up.

A stream of impressions came all at once. As I observed that the bedroom furniture was still in disarray and that, despite the open window, the air was still laced with the smell of spring cleaning—bleach, ammonia, methylated spirits, surprisingly pleasant— another image slotted in beneath the ceiling beams. Not all that striking an image: the same room, with all the furniture back in place and me by the dresser, studying my face in the mirror. And there behind me was Ton, alive and well, pressing button after button through the little loops on my 1920s taffeta dress.

I examined myself in the mirror. A bundle of nerves. The storm about to break. My lifelong fear of thunder and lightning. The sickening thud of my heart in the back of my throat. And all the while his fingers, dead calm, wrapping me, stroking the taffeta and the skin beneath, knowing exactly how to make me feel my own body.

But I shivered, took hold of his fingers, nibbled and then kissed them.

"What's the matter?" he asked.

I asked him what the time was.

"How come? It's not even nine. We've ages yet."

I hung around his neck. Whispered in his ear. Couldn't we just stay at home?

Tenderness, amusement in his eyes. The storm tearing loose at that same moment. He turned my face toward it, and yes, it was beautiful. Windows open wide. But my eyes were drawn to the merest twitch, imperceptible I knew to anyone but me, as his eyebrows creased together.

Before the first clap of thunder, I was under the covers, dress, shoes, and all. And Ton was lying beside me, also fully clothed. What did we care? He pressed my body to his. "You're overreacting," he said softly and I laughed because it was true.

My God, the open windows. And all the lights still on. Not to mention the iron. Electricity pulls lightning from the air. From under the bedclothes, I peered out at those flashes of quivering blue. How would it feel to be touched by one, pricked in the back by a finger of ten thousand Fahrenheit? To melt, to char in a loving embrace that never ends. Hands slid the flimsy fabric from my shoulders, my arms, skillfully undoing the buttons they had only just fastened. But the skirt remained in place, it had to, had to be part of this, along with the gossamer-thin slip relished by the pair of searching hands that were already stirring up visions. "Why the kid gloves?" I whispered. He smiled and rasped his unshaven chin hard across my cheek. We belong to each other. We are passionately in love, as if that wasn't clear enough. The sheets twisted along with our bodies, got in the way, trapping my legs, and we began to edge them down, shoes still on. Our heads bumped. I raised my eyes and looked into a pair of gleaming, slate-gray irises. The full length of him on top of me, tied and bound it seemed, and I knew he was out to imprint the weight of his body on me for good.

The storm beat a hasty retreat. One flash, then another, and I heard it stumble off into the distance like a stricken heifer. In the fever of a pleasure I had never known, I lay beneath my husband, my breath as shallow as I could make it. He grew heavier and I bore his weight proudly. Or tried to.

The telephone rang. A slap in the face. For although I was able to dive for the receiver and stop the racket—it was Lucia, and she began nattering away immediately—I could not stop the moment I had just inhabited from wrenching itself from me. From breaking off and floating away in time.

Yawning till the tears came, like I always seem to do when life confounds me, I heard Lucia say she had been invited to stay with friends in Groningen. Did I want to come along?

"Yes," I said hurriedly, eyes resting on the torn diary page beside the phone.

She asked me again.

"Yes! Yes, I'll come," I said. "I'd love to!"

There was a moment's silence.

"What's up?" I heard her say. "Are you ill?"

"No. Just very sleepy."

I realized she was used to coaxing me round. But I had no time to lose. Yes, fine! Now go, please! With any luck I might still be able to plunge back in where I left off.

Instead, I must have fallen into a deep sleep. One that lasted hours, the dreamless kind. I woke up staring into darkness, the lantern outside glinting in one of the linen-closet mirrors. My white housecoat shone blue. The memory of what had overcome me that afternoon was vivid. I knew it had been real and not a dream. There was enough corroborating evidence. I remembered the smell—still hanging in the air—the purple, storm-lit sky that had triggered the whispering, the lovemaking, the tangle of sheets. Above all, I remembered being in love. That, too, remained.

Only one thing confused me. Whatever I had experienced that afternoon, it had been in the company of a stranger. For I had never known a man who knotted his eyebrows with a telltale twitch. I had never gazed into indefinable, slate-gray eyes at such close quarters.

I nodded.

We had to step aside on the forest path to let a couple pass in the opposite direction. The man and the girl looked at us but seemed lost in themselves. They did not return our hellos.

"So you know, too," I said. "What that circle of silent people at the water's edge means."

He did not answer right away.

"Yes," he said at last. "I stood among them once."

The path widened again. Carrying the same image in our minds, both aware of its nature, we walked on side by side.

Late afternoon. When the sunbathers take one last dip in the sea. Dizzy from lying down, drunk from the heat. On North Sea beaches, the rising tide comes with channels and currents that can sweep you out to sea. The rescue teams know to be extra alert around that time. The drowning hour.

I had seen them at work. Rolling the body, heavy and limp as a fish, pressing down on the back, folding and lifting the arms. To the best of my recollection, the miracle always occurred. The eyes opened, the body rose on its elbows in stunned surprise, and asked for a cigarette.

One evening there was no circle, only a huddle of people looking out to sea. Waiting for a lifeboat to return, knowing the body had gone undiscovered. Close to shore, three crewmen jumped into the water, lifted the outboard motor, and dragged the sloop onto the sand. I can still see their faces. Men who had lived through the moment of no longer believing in their search.

Then came the time when I woke at first cock-crow with his name on my lips. With the untidy sense of expectation known to young animals and unsound minds. I began to dress to his taste. He had never told me which blouse he liked to see me wear but, empathizing with his gaze, I soon became adept at accentuating the line of my body. I discovered a perfume that would have tugged at his senses. I noted that the black T-shirt with the oval neck allowed the flat, gold chain to rest undisturbed against my collar bone.

I took good care of my youth. My twenty-five

years. I felt that I had to secure their future. If I did not, who would be around to love him later? And so I took to pulling on a pair of shiny cotton shorts and running through the woods in the early morning. As you push past the boundaries of tiredness, sometimes you see things with great clarity. The beauty of our relationship. The mystery. Of tree trunks in the morning mist. Of the blood pounding just behind my ears. Our love had been perfectly simple. Nothing shameful had taken place between us.

At school I knocked over my coffee at breaktime, breezed past the cleaner with a radiant smile, allowed an uneasy silence to linger during conversations with parents. "Who's the lucky guy?" Lucia said to me one day. "The whole village thinks you're in love."

I was in love. And by being in love, I was bringing my husband back from the dead, bringing him back to life. Was it so strange that, with nothing else to hand, I chose to bestow my emotions on a silent phantom? At night in bed, I spread my legs, caressed the extraordinary need of this love. I could feel the transfer of warmth from my body to his and knew he could no longer snigger at me, silent in his satin-lined coffin. Ton had been completely crazy about me. And I began to think of us as a single being. A touching, awkward, and—given the whimsical nature of our attraction—rather pitiful creature.

In August I woke up one night to the sound of a mosquito dancing around the room. I lay there listening to the muted whine for minutes on end before I realized I was shivering. I got up and closed the windows, then rummaged in the linen closet and pulled out the old quilted nightdress I would wear when I felt a cold coming on. I crawled back into bed. Eyes wide open, and about time, too. At last I was ready to break my lover's vow, the solemn, mutual promise I alone had kept, both before and after my husband's death.

My husband had loved someone else.

Months of wet weather must have followed. For, thinking back, there was always rain in the comments that the outside world inflicted on me and the various forms of obsession that brought me comfort. After a weekend spent locked away with my jealousy, bitterly angry that there was no longer any point in calling the one or two men I knew who might have helped me cheat on my husband, all my colleagues had to say come Monday morning was "For heaven's sake, put on a raincoat on a day like this!" And when I came to, after fainting in the supermarket—the checkout girl had been taking her time and I had been in a hurry, impatient to be alone with thoughts of how to eliminate, yes kill, the man who had abandoned me long before I'd had the chance to be a proper wife—the only response the locals could muster was to shove a stranger's dripping black umbrella into my hands at the exit.

"What were you thinking, ma'am? Out in this weather without anything to keep the rain off?"

I wanted to know who she was, this secret love. That meant dragging the box of papers and photos back down from the attic and, perched on the edge of my bed, sifting through them with a very different purpose. In my determination to find her, my gaze was mostly cool and dispassionate. Seldom did I admit, though I knew damn well, that I was a pathetic individual, humiliated by my own ritual and deeply ashamed of myself. And so it was that one day I happened upon a group photo.

I knew as soon as I saw her. There, with Ton, at the back of a group of students posing outside a university building. Broad smiles. Arms thrown around shoulders. There had been cause for celebration. Which made it all the more conspicuous that two of the gang were standing side by side, yet remained aloof. They were not touching, she and Ton. I picked up the magnifying glass from the table and studied the girl's face for a while. Round features, eyes without pretense, and something indomitable in the way she pressed her lips together. Was I coming to know something real and true about Ton for the first time? I took a deep breath, in and out. Relief. Perhaps my jealousy had not completely faded, but my anger had. I liked her. It wouldn't have bothered me all that much.

Days passed before I finally got Hugo Kakebeke on the line. Having recognized him in the photo, I had found my informant. At the student lodgings on Pietersteeg they kept insisting they had never heard of him. Nor did the names Dela and Milou Neefjes ring any bells. It was only when I refused to let up that they managed to dredge up a young man who, after a good deal of reluctant fumbling, supplied me with a telephone number. It was Thursday before Hugo

Kakebeke deigned to pick up the phone. He hadn't changed. After exchanging hellos, his first words were "Dear God, this rain! Is it as grim up north as it is down here?"

One week later, I found myself amid blocks of brand-new houses in Leiden, checking the name by the door. A door that showed no sign of opening. An hour later and I was back, staring at the nameplate, complete with his title and three initials. Again, no trace of him. At a loss, I wandered into town, walking familiar streets bereft of familiar faces. It was Friday evening and the cafés and bars were full to bursting. Leaning on an imitation marble tabletop, shoulder-to-shoulder with two men in leather jackets, I sat nursing a ludicrous cup of hot chocolate. I didn't even like the stuff. Lips smudged on tacky porcelain. The men joked as they left, sighing that it was time to head out and get rained on again. Good idea. For me, it was either head to the station and catch the first northbound train, stick around for pancakes, or eat something Greek. I went for Greek. The owner dragged a single table out from a row just for me, and presented a greasy, handwritten menu. Squid, eggplant, or yogurt with garlic. I ordered squid *and* yogurt with garlic, while eavesdropping on an intriguing conversation at the big table next to me. Something about a pianist who had lost his right arm in World War One.

Motel Cécile had a room for the night. I ran a bath and finally managed to squeeze a drop of delightful orange blossom oil from a foil packet into the water. I looked at my face in the washbasin mirror and saw, deep in the background, a cozy, quiet bedroom, and a bed with the covers turned down. What more could a body ask for? Should I go to sleep at once or lie back and ponder first?

I skipped the lying back and pondering. As I slid between the sheets and clicked off the light, I resolved to take an early train home. This madness had to end.

The next morning on the tram to the station, I spotted Hugo Kakebeke. He was sitting two rows in front of me, engrossed in his newspaper. I got up and edged my way toward him.

"What happened to you yesterday?" I asked, not quite able to contain my irritation.

He insisted that our appointment was for *this* afternoon at five, and that a wild duck had been marinating in my honor since last night.

I was taken aback. It was less than a year since I had seen him last, yet here I was gazing down on the benign face of a male in middle age, a foundation on which he was clearly going to build for the next forty years. I had always wondered when it began, as a gradual transition or—

I showed him the photograph.

Passengers squeezed past me, damp and dripping.

It took a while for the name to come to him. Linda! That was it. Linda—give me a sec—Passchier. He looked up at me in surprise, then looked away. He disapproves of what I'm doing, I thought, or perhaps he's just not a fan of being cornered on an early morning tram. I continued my inquiries regardless, but it turned out that he had known her only vaguely. The same went for Ton, or so he said. She had dropped out after the first year.

I got off at the next stop.

She was nice.

Every bit as nice as I'd thought she would be. We sat by the fire in her studio; the university dropout had become a photographer. I have always loved places where people work. The stable, the wash houses, the chicory greenhouse with the heavy curtain that plunged the roots into their familiar darkness. And now here, with Linda: bare floorboards, walls crammed with photographs, a thicket of mysterious racks, the white expanse of two open umbrellas.

Would you like tea? she had asked. Yes, I would. Lovely, thanks. She stood with her back to me, rummaging at a washstand in the corner. Firm legs, slippered feet. Attractive blond curls. She turned to look at me and smiled, top lip lifting to reveal a row of big, beautiful teeth. It was open, tender, the way she smiled. No, I wouldn't have minded. I held out the photo to her. She peered at it. Ah, good times! Half the class had failed their first-year exams and, of course, she'd been one of them. She remembered Ton vaguely, a red-haired boy, bright, cheerful. She had borrowed his notes once ahead of a tough assignment and their accuracy had left her feeling deflated. Whatever became of him?

He was dead.

Then I asked her if she had a car. Yes, she did, same one for years. As far back as Thursday, March 2, 1971? I asked. On the verge of laughter, she looked me in the eye and my neutral expression gave her pause for thought. She pressed her lips together. No, of course not. In her student days, she had zipped around on a moped, a Solex that did twenty, tops. She still missed it sometimes.

It was close to six when I left. We parted as friends. I was welcome anytime, she said.

The bus wound its way north. A stop in every village, which for the driver simply meant slowing down and speeding up again at this late hour. Few people felt the need to brave the evening rain.

Three villages on, I was the sole passenger. Sitting above the wheels, I heard the water hiss beneath my feet. In the rearview mirror I caught the watchful eyes of the driver, a colossal, dark-skinned man who was practically wedged behind the wheel. I lit up a smoke and let tiredness wash over me.

I knew that it was over. Ton, my silent guide on a journey to nowhere, had brought me to this destination. I would never know who he had been. I was not his widow. I was the widow of this bus journey in the rain, of the toothy girl with the tender smile, of the dark-skinned driver steering me home.

I took a slow drag on my cigarette and looked out at the sleeping farms.

When the church bell clangs in the distance, I stand still and count. Six o'clock. I have made it through the night. Fully conscious. Wiped out. Walking has failed to calm me this time. And though this man's coat has kept my body warm, my feet are cold as stone. Not exactly wise to pace the floor barefoot while an icy draft blasts through the baseboards. In the dark, my fingers feel for the ashtray on the table. I bump into the edge and hear it slide away from me. I take his last cigarette from the pack and switch on the light.

Blinded in my own living room. This comfortable

space with its plants, cushions, and paintings. In the corner lies Anatole, head resting on his front paws. Eyes cast upward, he is trying to gauge my aberrant behavior. The table has not been cleared. The dessert plates are still there, the mocha cups, the sugar bowl. Even the casserole dish failed to make it back to the kitchen after dinner. It was eleven by the time I placed the vodka on the table. There had been a silence then. We had stared at each other.

It had begun as the walk ended. I wanted to go home because I wanted him. I had a body, I could do with it as I pleased, and it pleased me to live life to the fullest. The way it should be lived. I spied my car and broke into a run. But when he caught up with me and, as if I had yelled instructions at him, grabbed me by the arm, spun me around, and pressed my face to his—narrow red nose, lean, clownish features, up close—I wriggled free.

"Let's go home," I said. "I'm freezing."

And I pulled off my gloves, held out my yellow-white fingers, and—oh Christ!—he took hold of my hand, and kissed them. The only thing missing was an "if I may be so bold ..."

"Look at the state of them," I mumbled to defuse the moment. "No feeling left at all."

We reached home and—no, once again I deferred. Even though I knew that, rattled by the nerve-racking

ritual of acquaintance, the best thing to do was sur-
render to the stranger's mouth and arms as soon as
the moment was ripe. Yet there I was, crouched by the
hearth, holding a match to a pyramid of kindling. It
caught fire at once, and I told him where he could find
the port. Then came dinner and oh, how we talked.

"Do you hear from her often?" he asked. I had told
him that, for the past two years, Lucia had been working at the racetrack in Sydney.

I shook my head, reluctant to pursue the topic.

"No," I said. "Never."

At the time, she had sent word of her arrival on
that other continent. After that, nothing.

He asked if I knew why she had wanted to move so
far away. I shrugged. God only knows.

I pulled the salad bowl toward me, picked up the
fork and spoon, and began tossing the leaves. "I put a
little sugar in the dressing," I informed him.

There was something perverse in my determination to keep happiness at bay, though for hours I had
felt it darting around me like a stray dog. We climbed
the stairs, I put the two slender glasses down by the
bedside lamp and strode into the bathroom. There I
snapped on the harsh light, brushed my teeth, rubbed
cream on my cheeks, drummed my fingers against my
eye sockets, and, by the time I slid fragrant and naked
into his arms, my exaltation had turned to agitation.

There we lay, grappling until he was on top of me, looking me in the eye, defiantly, indulgently. He had understood that I wanted this tussle, we have been together for years, and as I think this, something makes me hate him from the bottom of my heart. Makes me scream that I don't want him anymore, that he's gone too far, that I will never forgive him, never. I could spit in his face, drag my nails down his back. I feel the threat in his muscles, a man of flesh and blood, capable of anything, angry, seized by his own depths of rage. I am pushed down hard, onto my back—sure, why not, let him get on with it, let him—but my fury came to its senses. And my hands began to touch this man's warm, familiar body.

Once, on a winter's day, I met a young man with red hair and his sister's checkered scarf around his neck. We went skating together, fell through the ice somewhere near Hoogmade, and something tucked away among these simple facts must have led us to begin a relationship that lasted until the senseless crack of a pistol shot.

The night holds still now. Hesitates. I do not know if I can go on like this. Meet and tell, meet and tell. Chasing down the facts, hounding them in the hope that one day they might make the wrong move and dodge down a dead-end alley. Where I can corner them, search them, strip them of their smuggled goods.

I no longer hear a train, a dog howling. I look at the cinders in the hearth, still warm no doubt. The cigarette butts in the ashtray, the rims of the cups and glasses—they, too, must still be warm, sticky from my lips and the lips of the sleeping man upstairs. I would rather the tears did not come, but it occurs to me that maybe it was love after all. True and, in theory, for all time. That Ton and I honestly did love one another. Without much of a song and dance, perhaps, but still ... And that this was something, in the absent way we live from day to day, that I honestly believed.

The cold in my feet has become unbearable. Dancing with pain, I climb the stairs.

This time he snaps awake. For a moment I see him blank and bewildered. Then I see him realize where he is and with whom. The room, the bed, the brown coat that glides from my shoulders and onto the floor. He holds the covers open for me, and I slide into the glowing warmth.

And just as I am about to ask him, for no particular reason, about everything that has remained unasked and unspoken since yesterday—"When she threw the vacuum cleaner at you, you know, when you were asleep, did it actually hit you?"—an infernal noise erupts downstairs.

He looks at me dumbfounded.

"What the hell is that?"

Even I have to listen for a moment before I realize the kitchen timer has gone off.

I wrestle free of his arms.

"Time to take the Bundt cake out of the oven."

Exposed by Jean-Philippe Blondel

A French teacher on the verge of retirement is invited to a glittering opening that showcases the artwork of his former student, who has since become a celebrated painter. This unexpected encounter leads to the older man posing for his portrait. Possibly in the nude. Such personal exposure at close range entails a strange and troubling pact between artist and sitter that prompts both to reevaluate their lives. Blondel, author of the hugely popular novel The 6:41 to Paris, evokes an intimacy of dangerous intensity in a tale marked by profound nostalgia and a reckoning with the past.

The 6:41 to Paris by Jean-Philippe Blondel

Cécile, a stylish 47-year-old, has spent the weekend visiting her parents outside Paris. By Monday morning, she's exhausted. These trips back home are stressful and she settles into a train compartment with an empty seat beside her. But it's soon occupied by a man she recognizes as Philippe Leduc, with whom she had a passionate affair that ended in her brutal humiliation 30 years ago. In the fraught hour and a half that ensues, Cécile and Philippe hurtle towards the French capital in a psychological thriller about the pain and promise of past romance.

The Goose Fritz by Sergei Lebedev

This revelatory novel tells the story of a young Russian, the sole survivor of a once numerous clan of German origin, who delves relentlessly into an unresolved past. His ancestor migrated in the 1830s to the Russian Empire to practice alternative medicine and his descendants live through through centuries of turmoil during which none can escape their adoptive country's cruel fate. The Goose Fritz illuminates personal and political history in a passion-filled family saga about an often confounding country that has long fascinated the world.

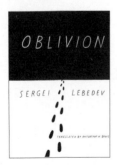

Oblivion by Sergei Lebedev

In one of the first 21st century Russian novels to probe the legacy of the Soviet prison camp system, a young man travels to the vast wastelands of the Far North to uncover the truth about a shadowy neighbor who saved his life, and whom he knows only as Grandfather II. Emerging from today's Russia, where the ills of the past are being forcefully erased from public memory, this masterful novel represents an epic literary attempt to rescue history from the brink of oblivion.

THE YEAR OF THE COMET BY SERGEI LEBEDEV

A story of a Russian boyhood and coming of age as the Soviet Union is on the brink of collapse. Lebedev depicts a vast empire coming apart at the seams, transforming a very public moment into something tender and personal, and writes with stunning beauty and shattering insight about childhood and the growing consciousness of a boy in the world.

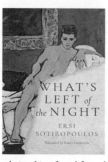

WHAT'S LEFT OF THE NIGHT
BY ERSI SOTIROPOULOS

Constantine Cavafy arrives in Paris in 1897 on a trip that will deeply shape his future and push him toward his poetic inclination. With this lyrical novel, tinged with an hallucinatory eroticism that unfolds over three unforgettable days, celebrated Greek author Ersi Sotiropoulos depicts Cavafy in the midst of a journey of self-discovery across a continent on the brink of massive change. A stunning portrait of a budding author—before he became C.P. Cavafy, one of the 20th century's greatest poets—that illuminates the complex relationship of art, life, and the erotic desires that trigger creativity.

THE EYE BY PHILIPPE COSTAMAGNA

It's a rare and secret profession, comprising a few dozen people around the world equipped with a mysterious mixture of knowledge and innate sensibility. Summoned to Swiss bank vaults, Fifth Avenue apartments, and Tokyo storerooms, they are entrusted by collectors, dealers, and museums to decide if a coveted picture is real or fake and to determine if it was painted by Leonardo da Vinci or Raphael. *The Eye* lifts the veil on the rarified world of connoisseurs devoted to the authentication and discovery of Old Master artworks.

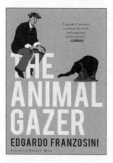

THE ANIMAL GAZER BY EDGARDO FRANZOSINI

A hypnotic novel inspired by the strange and fascinating life of sculptor Rembrandt Bugatti, brother of the fabled automaker. Bugatti obsessively observes and sculpts the baboons, giraffes, and panthers in European zoos, finding empathy with their plight and identifying with their life in captivity. Rembrandt Bugatti's work, now being rediscovered, is displayed in major art museums around the world and routinely fetches large sums at auction. Edgardo Franzosini recreates the young artist's life with intense lyricism, passion, and sensitivity.

ALLMEN AND THE DRAGONFLIES
BY MARTIN SUTER
Johann Friedrich von Allmen has exhausted his family fortune by living in Old World grandeur despite present-day financial constraints. Forced to downscale, Allmen inhabits the garden house of his former Zurich estate, attended by his Guatemalan butler, Carlos. This is the first of a series of humorous, fast-paced detective novels devoted to a memorable gentleman thief. A thrilling art heist escapade infused with European high culture and luxury that doesn't shy away from the darker side of human nature.

THE LAST WEYNFELDT BY MARTIN SUTER
Adrian Weynfeldt is an art expert in an international auction house, a bachelor in his mid-fifties living in a grand Zurich apartment filled with costly paintings and antiques. Always correct and well-mannered, he's given up on love until one night—entirely out of character for him—Weynfeldt decides to take home a ravishing but unaccountable young woman and gets embroiled in an art forgery scheme that threatens his buttoned up existence. This refined page-turner moves behind elegant bourgeois facades into darker recesses of the heart.

ADUA BY IGIABA SCEGO
Adua, an immigrant from Somalia to Italy, has lived in Rome for nearly forty years. She came seeking freedom from a strict father and an oppressive regime, but her dreams of film stardom ended in shame. Now that the civil war in Somalia is over, her homeland calls her. She must decide whether to return and reclaim her inheritance, but also how to take charge of her own story and build a future.

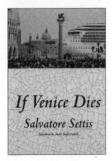

IF VENICE DIES BY SALVATORE SETTIS
Internationally renowned art historian Salvatore Settis ignites a new debate about the Pearl of the Adriatic and cultural patrimony at large. In this fiery blend of history and cultural analysis, Settis argues that "hit-and-run" visitors are turning Venice and other landmark urban settings into shopping malls and theme parks. This is a passionate plea to secure the soul of Venice, written with consummate authority, wide-ranging erudition and élan.

THE MADONNA OF NOTRE DAME
BY ALEXIS RAGOUGNEAU

Fifty thousand people jam into Notre Dame Cathedral to celebrate the Feast of the Assumption. The next morning, a beautiful young woman clothed in white kneels at prayer in a cathedral side chapel. But when someone accidentally bumps against her, her body collapses. She has been murdered. This thrilling novel illuminates shadowy corners of the world's most famous cathedral, shedding light on good and evil with suspense, compassion and wry humor.

THE MADELEINE PROJECT
BY CLARA BEAUDOUX

A young woman moves into a Paris apartment and discovers a storage room filled with the belongings of the previous owner, a certain Madeleine who died in her late nineties, and whose treasured possessions nobody seems to want. In an audacious act of journalism driven by personal curiosity and humane tenderness, Clara Beaudoux embarks on *The Madeleine Project*, documenting what she finds on Twitter with text and photographs, introducing the world to an unsung 20th century figure.

MOVING THE PALACE BY CHARIF MAJDALANI

A young Lebanese adventurer explores the wilds of Africa, encountering an eccentric English colonel in Sudan and enlisting in his service. In this lush chronicle of far-flung adventure, the military recruit crosses paths with a compatriot who has dismantled a sumptuous palace and is transporting it across the continent on a camel caravan. This is a captivating modern-day Odyssey in the tradition of Bruce Chatwin and Paul Theroux.

ON THE RUN WITH MARY
BY JONATHAN BARROW

Shining moments of tender beauty punctuate this story of a youth on the run after escaping from an elite English boarding school. At London's Euston Station, the narrator meets a talking dachshund named Mary and together they're off on escapades through posh Mayfair streets and jaunts in a Rolls-Royce. But the youth soon realizes that the seemingly sweet dog is a handful; an alcoholic, nymphomaniac, drug-addicted mess who can't stay out of pubs or off the dance floor. *On the Run with Mary* mirrors the horrors and the joys of the terrible 20th century.

THE LAST SUPPER BY KLAUS WIVEL

Alarmed by the oppression of 7.5 million Christians in the Middle East, journalist Klaus Wivel traveled to Iraq, Lebanon, Egypt, and the Palestinian territories to learn about their fate. He found a minority under threat of death and humiliation, desperate in the face of rising Islamic extremism and without hope their situation will improve. An unsettling account of a severely beleaguered religious group living, so it seems, on borrowed time. Wivel asks, Why have we not done more to protect these people?

GUYS LIKE ME BY DOMINIQUE FABRE

Dominique Fabre, born in Paris and a life-long resident of the city, exposes the shadowy, anonymous lives of many who inhabit the French capital. In this quiet, subdued tale, a middle-aged office worker, divorced and alienated from his only son, meets up with two childhood friends who are similarly adrift. He's looking for a second act to his mournful life, seeking the harbor of love and a true connection with his son. Set in palpably real Paris streets that feel miles away from the City of Light, a stirring novel of regret and absence, yet not without a glimmer of hope.

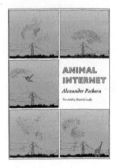

ANIMAL INTERNET BY ALEXANDER PSCHERA

Some 50,000 creatures around the globe—including whales, leopards, flamingoes, bats and snails—are being equipped with digital tracking devices. The data gathered and studied by major scientific institutes about their behavior will warn us about tsunamis, earthquakes and volcanic eruptions, but also radically transform our relationship to the natural world. Contrary to pessimistic fears, author Alexander Pschera sees the Internet as creating a historic opportunity for a new dialogue between man and nature.

New Vessel Press

To purchase these titles and for more information
please visit newvesselpress.com.